# A MIDSUMMER DREAM

Victoria Williams is photographing wildlife on the Cornish cliffs when she meets Bron Macdonald and becomes drawn into his world of film-making. During the shooting of an old Cornish legend, Vicky's integrity is threatened by a woman's jealousy. Seemingly insuperable obstacles arise between her and Bron, but are resolved. However, despite their reconciliation, Vicky must choose between loyalty to her sister and her love for Bron. How will she resolve her dilemma? Must she let Bron go?

Books by Janet Thomas
in the Linford Romance Library:

THE TIDES OF TIME
SUMMER SOJOURN
THE DANCING MAIDENS
THE OLD SUMMERHOUSE
SHADOWED LOVE
YESTERDAY'S SECRETS
CORNISH QUEST

JANET THOMAS

# A MIDSUMMER DREAM

### Complete and Unabridged

## LINFORD
*Leicester*

First published in Great Britain in 2009

First Linford Edition
published 2010

British Library CIP Data

Thomas, Janet, *1936 Oct. 24* –
    A midsummer dream. - -
    (Linford romance library)
    1. Wildlife photographers- -Fiction.
    2. Cornwall (England: County)- -Fiction.
    3. Love stories. 4. Large type books.
    I. Title II. Series
    823.9′14–dc22

    ISBN 978–1–44480–113–2

Published by
F. A. Thorpe (Publishing)
Anstey, Leicestershire

Set by Words & Graphics Ltd.
Anstey, Leicestershire
Printed and bound in Great Britain by
T. J. International Ltd., Padstow, Cornwall

This book is printed on acid-free paper

# 1

I had passed close to the cottage several times on my way down to the cove and seen the old man who lived there. Not quite closely enough to speak, but enough to notice that he seemed to live alone. He'd raise a hand when he was sitting outside his front door smoking a pipe, or tending the small patch of stony ground at the back where he grew vegetables and kept a few hens. I'd always thought what an inhospitable spot it was to live, swept by every wind that blew, but the waves booming in the caves below, and the blue infinity of sea and sky had a wild and rugged splendour all their own. The cottage was tucked back into the cliff and built low to withstand the gales, with a few feathery tamarisk trees on its most exposed side.

Today though, I noticed there was a

silver-grey Volvo parked in the lane and a much younger man was cutting the square of rough turf in front of the house using an ancient 'push me-pull me' lawn mower. He glanced up and smiled as I passed above him on the stony track which led down to the beach, and I caught a glimpse of tousled blond hair topping a narrow face with a wide and generous mouth.

I smiled back and hefted my camera and equipment higher up my shoulder as I turned my attention to negotiating the treacherous cliff-path. Two-thirds of the way down was a broad grassy ledge where I settled myself to wait.

Golden samphire was growing nearby in crevices among the rocks, as was the rarer sea-lavender. The mauve and gold of the flowers against the azure sea and slate-grey rock was magnificent and I angled my lens to try and capture its beauty before the light changed. August had started well and so far it had been a glorious spell of dry weather, during which I'd been taking as many outdoor exposures as possible.

And I was hoping for some more today. I turned and wriggled onto my stomach as I focused the camera on the colony of grey seals far below in the rocky cove. And waited some more.

\* \* \*

'Fascinating creatures, aren't they?' I jumped feet at the unexpected voice, the camera jerked and my carefully set-up shot was ruined. Ruined — after sprawling on the edge of the cliff, after painstakingly getting it lined up, and after waiting all that time to get it absolutely right! I swore, scrambled to my feet and whirled round to glower at the young man who was standing behind me, the one who had been mowing the grass. Hands in his pockets, he stood nonchalantly looking over the sea whistling a tune to himself, apparently totally unaware of what he had just done.

'Are you really as stupid as you

seem?' I flung at him, feeling colour flood my face as my voice rose up the scale in fury and frustration. 'I've been waiting for the best part of the afternoon to get a shot of that female seal suckling her pup, but she's been in the water until ten minutes ago. And then, at the very moment when they were exactly right, you have to come along and ruin it! Now she's going back again, look! I'll never get another opportunity like that.' I could hear my voice rising to a wail, and had to forcefully swallow down a lump in my throat that was threatening tears born out of sheer frustration.

'Hey,' he took a step back and put up both hands in defence, 'Look here — I'm sorry, sorry, sorry! I was watching them as well and didn't take too much notice of what you were up to. I thought you had binoculars there — not a camera.'

'You've no idea how important this is to me.' Still glaring, I snapped back. 'This is my work — it's what I do for a living! I haven't got time to hang around enjoying the view like some people. And there goes most of my day, wasted. Is it any wonder I blew up?'

His brows drew together in a frown, and the smile faded as steel grey eyes bored into mine. 'Hey, I've apologised, right? What more do you want — blood?' He gestured to the seals below. 'Look,' he pointed a finger, 'your precious female's coming back — she's changed her mind. You can get another take — but you were so busy laying into me you didn't even notice. So, who's wasting time now?'

I ran a hand through my hair and knew the short auburn crop would be standing on end, but all the anger was draining out of me. Because he was right. I'd made a fool of myself and over-reacted, hadn't I? To cover my confusion I turned my back on him and took up my original position, camera poised. About a dozen seals were drawn up onto the shingle now, like beached whales, and were basking within a few feet of the waves, and yes, he was right — infuriating man.

The female was heaving herself laboriously up the sloping beach towards her pup once more.

With difficulty I tried to ignore the hovering shadow behind me as I peered intently through the lens, then easily captured the shot I had wanted for so long. Several more followed and at last I had no excuse for sprawling there any longer. I wriggled backwards, put the camera down beside me on the grass and hoped that by now he would have gone. It was very quiet, so I stood up, turned round and jumped again, for there he still was. Standing just behind me like a statue, with his arms folded across his chest. 'Can I let my breath out now please?' he said with a suspicious twinkle in his eye. Was he making fun of me? I scowled back, but he only grinned. 'I've been holding it, in case I misbehave again,' he added.

'Idiot!' His expression was so comical as he turned his gaze skywards that I couldn't help but burst out laughing. The merriment seemed to blow away my anger as well as the restraint between us, and when he settled himself on a flat rock and patted the space beside him I hardly thought twice about joining him.

'I'm Bron Macdonald,' he said, extending a hand. He was actually turning out to be rather nice I thought, as I took it. 'Victoria Williams. I'm Vicky to my friends.'

'Oh, right, Vicky,' he replied pointedly, as our eyes met. He quirked an eyebrow in a friendly way as he asked, 'do you live locally or are you down here on holiday?'

Was he trying to chat me up? I might have told him to clear off and mind his own business if he wasn't looking at me with such an engaging smile. And he had one of those faces that you instantly trust on sight. Besides, how could one hedge around direct questions like these, anyway? So I smiled back. 'Yes, I live not far from here, in

Penzance with my sister. She keeps a second hand bookshop, and we have the flat above.'

'Ah,' he nodded, and before he could ask any more personal questions I got in with one of my own.

'Which part of Scotland do you come from?' I asked. The accent was unmistakable.

He gave a soft chuckle. 'A pretty remote part. Orkney in fact.'

'Oh?' Momentarily lost for words, for I had to rack my brains to remember where Orkney actually was, I recovered myself just in time before the pause became long enough for him to notice. Then, 'Orkney?' I said in astonishment. 'You're not joking, are you? That's about as remote as it gets! You couldn't be farther away and still be in Britain. A bit like down here. Land's End is only a stone's throw away, you know. What are you doing so far from home?'

Bron shrugged. 'Och, I don't live there now, it's where I was born and brought up. My parents are still in

Stromness though. I go back some-times. And we don't call ourselves Scots, you know,' he added. 'We're Orcadians.'

'Orcadians?' He had my interest now and I looked him full in the face. 'A bit like the Cornish, then. Many Cornish people don't consider themselves to be English either — Cornwall being a land in its own right.'

'Yes — I've heard that. Anyway, I've got a flat in London, which is my base. But it's only a base. At the moment I'm staying in the cottage up there with old Doug while we're filming.' He picked up a handful of pebbles and chinked them around in his palm.

'Filming?' I knew my eyes had widened. 'What kind of filming?'

Bron chuckled and tossed one of the stones over the edge as he replied, 'Oh, nothing like it sounds — I'm no Zeffirelli. I work for a regional group that's trying to involve local schools in their own folk culture.' He threw the rest of the stones after the first and dusted off his hands. 'You're looking puzzled.'

He must have noticed my frown. 'Yes, I don't really understand what you mean.'

'Oh, they want to make children aware of their heritage, you see,' Bron went on. 'They make sure they have story hours and interactive play and so on. At the moment I'm in Cornwall making films about local legends with some of them.' He spread his hands expressively to include the arc of the cove and the stark cliffs rising sheer from the ocean on either side.

'Oh, I see. That's really good,' I said, and meant it. 'What a wonderful idea.'

'Yes,' Bron replied. 'It's fun as well as work — when everything's going all right, that is. I've got a small group of actors to play out the stories, with the children as extras, but of course we do run into problems from time to time. Personality clashes, that sort of thing.' His expression darkened as he looked out to sea again.

Then the smile was back as he turned directly towards me and said, 'Speaking of work, you said that was what you're doing. Are you a professional photographer then?'

I nodded. 'Yes — freelance. At the moment I'm doing a series of wildlife shots for a printing firm for their calendar next year.' There was a pause before I added quietly, 'Which is why I was balancing on the edge of the cliff waiting for the seals to pose for me.' Shamefaced I glanced away and nibbled my bottom lip. 'I — I'm really sorry I lost my temper and shouted at you like that.' I had to explain. 'But I'd been stuck there for so long I was really fed up, and I took it out on you.'

'No problem,' Bron shrugged, 'and I apologise as well for startling you. I should have had more sense, but my thoughts were miles away.' He uncurled his lean form, rose to his feet and held out a hand to draw me up as well. 'So, no hard feelings?' he smiled.

'No hard feelings.' I shook my head

and as I looked up I felt the full force of his magnetic eyes. I'd thought at first they were grey, but now with the sun shining fully in his face they had changed to a brilliant sapphire blue.

'Do you get plenty of work then?' he was asking me, as I suddenly came back to earth.

'Oh — um — I can't complain, I suppose. I make a living, and I'm doing what I love, which is important, I think, don't you?'

'Oh absolutely,' Bron replied fervently. 'And I should know. I've done all sorts of boring jobs in my time, in order to make ends meet, just waiting for a break. Until at last I landed this contract with the Local Culture Foundation, which means I can do what I love, too, making films — at least for the foreseeable future. They're planning to go all over the country with this scheme.' He shrugged and that sudden smile lit up his narrow, intelligent face like a reflection of the sunlight around us. 'I guess we're just both creative people.'

'What exactly are you working on at the moment?' I asked.

'Oh, the legend of the Mermaid of Zennor. You know it of course.'

He quirked an eyebrow as I exclaimed, 'Oh yes. Having been born and bred around here, I should say so! Then you've obviously been in the church and seen the bench-end carved with her picture.'

'Oh yes, several times,' he replied. 'The mermaid who captured the heart of a young man and took him back with her to her home under the sea.'

Bron took a backwards step or two as he gazed towards the horizon, where now the dying rays of the sun were painting the sky with streaks of lemon and flame, as if he was looking for a gleam of golden hair, or the flick of a fishy tail.

I nodded and glanced at my watch as I realised that the sun was rapidly creeping down towards the west. I reached for my camera and bag, then as a mournful wail like the howling of a banshee came echoing up the steep sides of the cove I peered over the edge once more, then laughed. 'Did you hear that?' I asked. 'What a noise they make, don't they?'

Bron was standing beside me now, his tall jeans-clad figure dwarfing my own five foot six, and nodded. 'Like a soul in torment,' he replied with a smile. 'It would scare anyone stiff who didn't know what it was — especially after dark.'

'Which reminds me, I must be going,' I said. 'I've been far longer than I meant to be and it's quite a walk back to the car. I left it in the park near Carn Galver.'

'I needed more exercise than mowing that bit of grass, so I've been out for a good long hike,' Bron replied. 'But I'll walk part of the way back with you. If you don't mind, that is. You can tell me what sort of photographic equipment you use. I'd be interested to see all your stuff sometime. It must be kind of tricky catching wild life — plus you need a lot of patience. No wonder you yelled at me back there!'

I gave a rueful smile. 'Of course I don't mind,' I replied. Bron was turning out to be far more agreeable than I'd thought. He thrust his hands in his pockets as we began to move and I raised a hand to shade my eyes as I gazed back at the sea, where the sun was slipping towards the horizon in a huge orange ball.

We were climbing now, in single file up a tortuous track towards the main road. It was strewn with huge boulders of bed-rock which poked through the thin layer of soil and sparse grasses and put paid to conversation for a moment or two as we watched where we were putting our feet.

Then as it levelled out again I said, 'I've heard tales of fishermen that have sworn they've seen mermaids when they're at sea, and heard them singing. I'm sure though that they must have been seals — not that the noise they make is anything like singing!' Bron was walking beside me again as I went on, 'Seals have got such beautiful faces though, and they're really friendly creatures, you know.' He nodded.

I paused for a moment, wondering whether to tell him this or not. I'm not normally one for confiding my deepest feelings, especially to a stranger, but there was something about this man that invited confidences. So, 'I went swimming with a seal once,' I said softly. 'You did?' Bron's eyes widened.

'Yes. Well, a seal went swimming with me, actually,' I added. 'It was off the cove back there where we were just now, out beyond the rocks. I was on my own and suddenly this beautiful head popped up out of the water right beside me and looked straight into my face. It was the most wonderful experience I've ever had. It looked so intelligent, with those great soulful eyes they have, and it seemed to be smiling right at me.' I felt myself flush and looked down at my feet, waiting for him to laugh. But he didn't. When I looked up I found that he was gazing intently down at me.

'Fantastic,' he said. 'I think seals are just as intelligent as they look, don't you?'

I nodded and smiled with relief that he had understood. 'They're so awkward on land, aren't they though? The way you see them heaving their way down the beach, inch by inch. It looks such hard work. But as soon as they slide into the water, they're transformed.' I was remembering the agile bodies I'd been watching in the surf while I had been waiting for them to come up into the cove and settle.

'And they're very responsive to music — did you know that? There was a girl up in Scotland somewhere who used to take her violin down to the beach and practise, and the seals would come out of the water when they heard her.'

'Really?' I turned to him with interest. 'No, I hadn't heard that. I'll have to bring mine down here one day and see what happens. Maybe they'll get up on their tails and dance!'

Bron laughed, a deep-throated infectious chuckle, and I couldn't help joining in.

'So you play the violin?' he remarked, serious again and I shrugged. I hadn't meant to let that out.

'Oh, not very well. I don't practise enough. I used to be in the school orchestra years ago but I rarely play at all now.'

At that moment we arrived at the main road. 'This is where we part company, Bron.' I pointed. 'That's my car over there — the blue Fiesta.'

'Oh, right.' He hung around as I dug in my pocket for the keys and let myself into the vehicle, then said casually, 'Will you be coming down here again at all? Or have you finished with the seals now?'

'I'm not sure until I see how these shots turn out,' I called through the window as I started the engine.

'Come and see us down at Zennor sometime if you'd like to watch the filming. We'll be there for at least another two weeks.'

'I might do that,' I smiled and nodded as I let the clutch in, 'I'll see how the time goes. Bye.' He stood in the road and waved until I turned a corner and he was out of sight.

★　★　★

'I met a nice guy on the cliffs this afternoon,' I said casually to Diane my sister, as we sat in the kitchen eating a simple meal of cold chicken and salad. I couldn't seem to get him out of my mind — that magnetic smile, the blue, blue eyes.

'Oh?' Diane replied with interest, as her eyebrows rose. We shared the same auburn hair and hazel eyes inherited from our mother, who had died along with our father in the light aircraft which had been his passion. It came down after hitting a storm and had crashed into the side of a mountain in Wales. Diane had been twenty then and I six years younger.

'Well, I didn't think of him as nice at first — ' I laughed and waved a drumstick as I started telling Diane the whole story. 'Then he said why don't I go over to Zennor and watch them filming,' I finished, 'so I said I'd think about it.' Wiping my greasy fingers on a napkin, I pushed back my empty plate. 'That was good, Diane — I was so hungry.'

'You always are,' Diane chuckled. 'It must be all the fresh air that goes with the job. But you never put on weight however much you eat, do you?' she added with envy. Diane was always conscious of the calories.

'Anyway, how was your day?' I asked, knowing I was leaning inelegantly on my elbows and equally aware that I was too old now for her to tell me off as she used to.

'Surprisingly busy. You'd think all the visitors would be on the beach in this lovely weather, but we had a lot who came in looking for books on Cornwall, not only history but legends and folk-lore too. I made some good sales.'

'Perhaps they were some of Bron's crew,' I suggested. Diane raised her head from her plate to glance towards me. 'Oh, so it's Bron, is it?' That's an unusual name. 'Is it short for something?'

'I don't know — I didn't ask him. But I will.' I knew that she would have noticed the faraway look on my face. Having been mother, companion and friend to me for so many years, Diane knew me almost as well as I know myself. How long was it in fact? I did a mental check. About ten years now since the tragedy.

Diane had almost single-handedly, apart from the support at first of an elderly aunt and uncle, managed to acquire the book-shop which meant that she could work from home instead of in the local public library, and be there for me going to school, and the flat above it which replaced our former home when it had been sold. That house had been too full of memories for either of us to carry on living there.

During this time, Dave had turned up and swept Diane off her feet in a whirlwind romance. They had been married within months and he moved in with us. I was at the local polytechnic studying photography by then, and so totally wrapped up in myself and my own affairs that I was like the ostrich with its head in the sand.

When the marriage had broken down it had come as a total shock to me. I had failed to notice the cracks which must have been there for a while before Dave eventually walked away with another woman and out of Diane's life for ever.

Diane and I were close, but this was one subject which we never really talked about. With my new maturity however, I wondered guiltily whether my constant presence in their lives had been part of the trouble. I had plucked up enough courage to mention this to Diane on one occasion but she flatly denied it, so I was no further forward.

After the divorce and the initial outburst of shock at his betrayal she never mentioned Dave's name again, keeping her grief and anger to herself and continuing to provide a home for me.

I admired my sister's self-control immensely and I knew that she valued my company, but I did wonder sometimes how she would feel if I met someone special and wanted to move out. So far that had never happened — there had been casual relationships, but I was so bound up in my work that I didn't do a lot of socialising. Whether Diane would welcome the idea of having the flat to herself — or whether she liked having me around, was something I couldn't decide. I didn't even know why I was suddenly thinking like this anyway.

'So you're seeing him again, then?' Diane's voice broke in on my thoughts as she rose to take the plates to the kitchen.

'I told you — I'm going to watch

them filming,' I called towards her retreating back. 'Once I finish this job I'll take a few days off.'

I gathered up the belongings which I'd dropped on the floor when I came in, and took them down to my room. The flat was a sprawling affair, extending partly over the property next door, so that there were two good-sized bedrooms and a bathroom, as well as our kitchen and living room. Mine faced the sea, looking out over Mount's Bay, the sheer beauty of it never failing to soothe me after a hard day, or heighten my delight when something was going well. The steadfast and timeless presence of St. Michael's Mount had sustained me through the terrible years after the tragedy which had pitched me into an anguished adolescence, and had been in its way as comforting as an old friend.

Now, dusk was falling and the shadowy castle-crowned island seemed to float above the darkening water, as insubstantial as a fairytale. Stretching away into the distance to my left lay the blurred shape of the Lizard promontory, and to the right the lights had started to twinkle on the coast road beyond Penzance leading to the fishing villages of Newlyn and Mousehole.

★   ★   ★

A few days later I was thinking of trying for some shots of bird life for another page of the wild-life calendar, when I remembered how I'd been watching a buzzard riding the thermals while I was waiting for the seals the other day. The day I'd met Bron. Well, the great bird of prey would be a splendid subject, hunting on the open moors, perching on the rocky crags of the uplands around . . . Zennor, maybe?

# 2

A couple of days later I set off for Zennor, taking the steadily rising route towards St. Ives until at the fork just above the town I swung the car to the left and followed the dipping and twisting road that ran parallel to the coast.

Immediately I sensed the different feel to the surroundings here. Stark and savage, great boulders of unyielding granite piled in untidy heaps reared above my head, the last bastion of an ancient and primitive land. These precarious-looking carns threatened at any minute to tumble towards the sea, where far below on the level ground, tiny fields enclosed by dry-stone walls were spread out like a patchwork quilt drying in the sun.

The small hamlet of Zennor, little more than a church, a pub and a handful of cottages, lay in a cup-like depression slightly sheltered from the incessant wind which always blew around the exposed uplands. In one of the fields behind a farm just outside the village I could see a cluster of vehicles, trailers and camper vans, which I assumed was where the film crew had their base. My heart beat a little faster as I told myself I would do the job I had come to do, first, before going in that direction. But I was too late. As I parked the car and reached for my back-pack I heard a voice hailing me. A voice I recognised.

'Vicky! How lovely to see you again — and so soon.' It was Bron of course, crossing the car park with a load of his own gear. Not wanting him to think that I hadn't been able to keep away, I hastily replied, 'Oh, Bron. Yes, you too. But I'm actually working. I came over to get some shots of buzzards hunting. It's great country for them around here.'

He grinned and hoisted the bag he

was carrying further up his shoulder. 'Yeah — I saw a couple myself earlier. They were circling around the carn up that way. I watched them for a while. That's where you should go.' He jerked a thumb.

'Oh, right.' Today he was wearing a sweater of soft blue that exactly matched his eyes, with jeans that hugged his slim hips like a second skin. Suddenly realising how I was staring at him, I hastily added, 'Thanks. I will,' as I felt a wash of colour rise to my face.

'Well, come and have a look at the set when you're through. We'll be shooting all day. Must go now,' he half-turned and spoke over his shoulder, 'they're waiting for me.'

'OK, I'll do that. See you later.' I raised a hand and turned up the road towards the moor as Bron's long stride took him quickly down the lane and around a corner out of sight.

I crossed over and took the track leading up onto the open moor in the direction he had indicated. It was a steep climb and I had to watch my step as scattered boulders lurked everywhere, half-hidden in the undergrowth waiting to trip the unwary foot. Consequently, I didn't realise how high up I was until I paused to draw breath and looked back over my shoulder.

The view from here was breathtaking and I never ceased to marvel at it every time I came. The village had receded and taken on the dimensions of a child's toy. From where I stood on the brow of the hill I now had a clear view of both north and south coastlines, stretching from Mount's Bay on one side to Hayle and beyond, on the other. Easing my rucksack from my shoulders, I sat down on a comfortable boulder at the foot of a towering carn to drink it all in and take a brief rest. Then my heart lurched as I suddenly saw it. Perched on a jutting crag way above my head a buzzard was sitting, immobile as the rock itself, outlined against the perfect azure of the cloudless sky like a cardboard cut-out. It was haughtily surveying the landscape spread before it with unblinking yellow eyes, the cruel curved beak silhouetted against the sun.

There was no time to waste. Moving as slowly as I could I drew out my camera, holding my breath in case the movement should alert the great bird into flight, and on hands and knees crept a little closer up the rock pile towards it. Now I could see its great yellow talons, fully extended as it gripped its perch, and imagined them tearing into the flesh of some unfortunate small creature. What a contrast to the speckled softness of its breast feathers and the smart dark chestnut of its still folded wings. Still folded. I mentally crossed my fingers as I removed the lens cap and angled the camera. Thank goodness for digital — this was no time for fine tuning if I was to capture that perfect shot while I had the chance.

Got it! I let out the breath I didn't realise I'd been holding and took another photo, and another again, just as the great bird opened its wings and lazily launched itself upwards into the thermals. Then before it was carried way over the moor, it hovered motionless for just long enough, and I captured it again. Wonderful — what a stroke of luck. It was almost too good to be true. I mustn't gloat until I found out what the results were like, but I had the feeling they were going to be spectacular. I grinned as I eased myself upright and rubbed my aching knees, cramped from being in one position on the unyielding rock for so long and scraped where I had crawled around. I should have worn trousers instead of shorts. But it had been well worth it.

I know the smile stayed on my face all the way back, and I was grinning like an idiot, partly because of my successful trip and partly . . . yes, admit it, because I was going to see Bron again. How could this man have made such an impression on me in such a short time? I knew next to nothing about him, but he'd hardly ever been out of my mind since the day we'd met.

Now I felt a shiver of anticipation as the village came closer and the buildings regained their rightful size. From this angle I could see a knot of people gathered at the far side of the car park, outside the old chapel which had been converted into a back-packers hostel and café, and having locked away my camera in the boot of my own car, I strolled across to them.

Bron was standing on the fringe of the group, a coffee mug in his hand, and was deep in earnest conversation with a young woman of about my own age. Dark hair cut in a long bob, with still darker eyes and a haughty expression, she glanced at me with a calculating gaze as I drew nearer and gestured to Bron. He looked over his shoulder, his smile widening as our eyes met.

'Vicky! Come and meet everyone. It's a good time, we're just having a break. Pour yourself a coffee if you want — or a cold drink. Over there.' He pointed towards a trestle table on which stood several large jugs and a stack of mugs.

'Hi,' I gave a general nod and smile at the group. 'Thanks, Bron, I'd love one.'

When I returned, he started on the introductions. 'This is Vicky, folks, we met on the cliffs the other day and due to a — um — misunderstanding she was so annoyed with me that I thought she was going to push me over!'

'Oh, Bron, don't exaggerate — you're embarrassing me!' I protested as everybody laughed. Everybody except the dark girl who was still staring at me unabashed. 'This is Rebecca,' he said, and with only a slight lifting of her expression she extended the tips of her fingers to my outstretched hand.

'Over here we have Alexis,' Bron indicated a tall blonde, 'Jim at the back there is our chief camera-man and this is Andy who's on sound. Max is our leading man. The two youngsters over there,' he waved a hand towards a couple of children about eight and ten years old, 'are Isabel and her brother

Sam. There are few 'backup boys' around, but most of the others are extras, not here today — local people whom you'll get to know as we go along — if you're going to be around much, that is.' He raised an eyebrow and I nodded.

'I'd be really interested in watching,' I replied, 'if you're sure I shan't be in the way. I've finished all the photography for the calendar, so until I get another commission . . . ' I shrugged, 'I think I've earned some time off to spend in a good cause.'

'Great.' Bron upended his mug and drained it. 'Time for us to get back to work.' He clapped his hands for attention. 'Right, folks, positions again please. And Becca darling, do try a bit harder with the Cornish accent. I know it's not easy, but after all the time Sue spent coaching you, surely you must have some idea by now.'

'Oh Bron, don't be cross,' the red slash of her mouth drooped as she sidled up to him and laid a sinuous hand on his arm. Gazing up into his eyes she added, 'I'm doing the best I can, but it is hard.' He nodded and patted the small hand before he withdrew. The little scene spoke volumes. Well, what did I expect? That a man with such charisma wouldn't have a woman in his life? Get real, I told myself.

'Right. Back to the knoll everybody,' Bron said, leading the way to a small grassy hillock from which there was a view of the sea not far away. As Rebecca and the two children took up their places, Bron said in an aside to me, 'Rebecca's the narrator and has the only speaking part. She's supposed to be an old woman telling it the story to her grandchildren. There's no dialogue in the rest of it,' he explained briefly, his eyes on the cast, 'only background music to set the tone, and the actions of the characters themselves.'

'It sounds fascinating,' I replied, as Rebecca pulled a cloak around her shoulders and covered her hair with its hood. She sat with shoulders hunched like an old woman, with the children kneeling on either side of her, as Jim wheeled over the camera on its trolley and began to angle it into position. Careful to keep out of sight, Andy hovered in the background waving a microphone that resembled a huge fluffy sausage, as Rebecca began to speak.

'This is the first scene,' Bron whispered to me, then left my side to go and direct his actors.

'Well, once upon a time, my dears . . .' Rebecca began, 'there was a young man whose name was Matthew Trewhella. They called him Matty, and he was the most handsome man in the village and for miles around.' Rebecca raised a hand and indicated the panorama of sea and countryside. 'More than that, he could sing like an angel. No-one could equal his magnificent voice, and people would come from far and near to hear him sing in the church choir on Sundays. So the church was always full, which made the vicar very happy.'

'Right! Cut there,' Bron broke in. 'Andy, I need you to pan around more when Becca raises her hand — get in a sweep to the village and the church tower, then back to them.' He turned to the group of three and went on, 'That was slightly better, Rebecca, but you've still a long way to go before you sound like a local. We'll have to do it again. Now, concentrate.' She lowered her head and scowled at him.

But Bron was right. I'd been thinking myself just how awful her accent was, but could hardly say so. Any true Cornish person like me would have laughed out loud, it was so pseudo. It really irritated me to think that this film was going to be filed away in archives somewhere and people would think it was authentic. But . . . it was none of my business.

'OK. Ready for another take.' Bron held up one hand. 'And — action!' They went through the whole scene again. And once more after that, as

Bron found something else that needed ironing out. And still Rebecca's accent wavered somewhere between Scouse and Somerset. By this time I was getting bored, so goodness knows how those children remained so well-behaved — I admired their patience.

But at last Bron sighed and glanced at his watch. 'Right, thanks everybody — we'll break for lunch now.' He glanced at his watch. 'And I hope we can wind this one up this afternoon. We are working to a deadline you know.' He looked pointedly towards Rebecca. 'Shooting resumes in an hour.' Bron combed long fingers through his wind-swept hair and strolled over to me. 'Are you staying on, Vicky? Or have you had enough of us for one day?' A brief smile lifted some of the strain from his face, but he was still looking tired.

He'd discarded his sweater now that the sun was overhead and the white tee-shirt he was wearing accentuated the golden tan on his arms and face. He could have been a Viking hero, or a

Greek god . . . I pulled myself together with a jerk. 'I — I've got some sandwiches with me, Bron. I intended eating them up on the hill, not thinking I'd be through so early.'

'Great. The pub's supplying us with food — it's part of their contract.' He gestured with a hand. 'Along with the upstairs room there that we're hiring for changing in. So hang on while I go and grab something and then we can eat together. How about going back up to the carn? I need to get away from here for a proper break.'

'Well, yes, fine, I'd love to but . . . ' I hesitated and glanced over my shoulder towards Rebecca who was just entering the Tinners Arms, deep in conversation with Alexis, 'what about — um — your friends?'

Bron followed my line of vision and grinned. 'Oh, those two — a picnic out in the sun would be the last thing they'd want — too worried about their complexions you see. They'll be eating indoors. And Andy and Jim are best mates — they'll be having a beer together.'

My spirits lifted and I knew I had an answering grin on my own face. 'I'll just go and pick up some stuff — don't go away.' He loped off, swiftly covering the ground with his easy long-legged stride.

Bron was soon back, clutching a plastic carrier bag which he slung over one shoulder as we took the track across the road and climbed high onto the moor where I'd been working that morning.

'Phew! It's too hot to go much further — this'll be OK, won't it?' Bron indicated a nook in between two large hoary boulders and flung himself down on the short turf.

'Perfect.' I dropped my back-pack and settled on a cushion of springy heather beside him. A clump of brilliant pink foxgloves were growing nearby and the colour of their tall spires against the azure sky was fantastic. It had the photographer in me mentally reaching for the camera, but this time alone with

Bron was too precious to lose. So as we both tucked in to our lunch I said, 'So you'll have to go over that scene yet again this afternoon?'

'Ah,' he gave a sigh and leaned back against the rocks. 'Yes, I'm afraid so.' A frown crossed his face and the worry lines reappeared. 'I really do want to get that one in the can before we start on scene two, but I've arranged for all the extras to come in later, and I can't send them away. So I might have to leave it for the time and go back to it when Becca has perfected her dialect.'

'Cornish is notoriously difficult to get right if you weren't actually born to it,' I said.

Bron looked up. 'Vicky, you are, aren't you? Cornish-born I mean. Can you speak in dialect?' He gave me a calculating look.

'Well, ye-es,' I said guardedly, having an inkling of the way his train of thought was going. Bron's expression brightened. 'Maybe you could coach Rebecca as we go along.' The idea

41

didn't exactly hold instant appeal, but Bron had been so friendly that it put me in a difficult position.

I shrugged. 'I suppose so. If you think it would help.' Bron's face lit up with what looked like relief. 'Oh Vicky, thanks! It would, I'm sure it would.' He nibbled a thumbnail in thought. 'Then we might manage to get through it today after all.'

'And what happens in scene two?' I asked through a mouthful, changing the subject as I wondered what I'd let myself in for.

'Ah.' Bron took a swig of water from a large bottle at his side, 'scene two takes place inside the church.'

I felt my eyes widen. 'Inside? You're allowed to film in a church?'

He wiped the back of his hand across his mouth and screwed the top on the bottle. 'Yes, we've had special permission from the vicar. I think the village is so pleased to have our custom — we've spent quite a lot on this shoot, you see, that they're falling over themselves to back us up. Plus it'll be fantastic publicity for their holiday businesses too.'

I nodded. That made perfect sense. 'As I said, this is when we get all the extras in, to act the part of villagers coming to church on Sunday. Then we have 'Matty Trewhella' singing a solo, backed up by the choir, when the door opens again and this strange and beautiful woman comes in.' Bron's hands were waving all over the place as he tried to describe the picture in his mind. 'All heads turn,' he went on, 'as she walks down the aisle and takes a seat right in the front, fixing him with a unblinking stare. Matty falters, fluffs his words, then recovers himself, but can't look away from her. As if she's cast a spell on him, you see.'

'Which she has,' I remarked, and he nodded. 'It sounds wonderful,' I added, 'I'm really looking forward to seeing it.' I threw the remaining crumbs of my lunch to a waiting bird and leaned back, replete.

'Tell me about your group,' I said, fishing. 'How long have you all known each other?' Bron narrowed his eyes against the sun as he turned towards me. 'Oh, most of them only since I engaged them for this job. When the board gave me the contract, they let me have a free hand in forming my own company.' He swatted at a persistent wasp which was hovering around us, before going on.

'Jim's an old mate of mine, I knew his work from before, and he told me about Andy. But the girls answered the advertisement I put in the paper, as did Max. He and Alexis had done a bit of acting before, in repertory, but Becca's come to it cold. Apparently she's always fancied acting, but I get the impression that she had something more glamorous in mind than playing an aged crone covered up in a cloak.' He chuckled softly. 'But she's going along with it in case anything else comes up after this. She was working in make-up and manicure at a hair and beauty salon when she answered the advert.' He grinned. 'I guess that's why she takes such care of her skin!'

'And you?' I probed. 'What did you do before?' Bron looked away and the set of his jaw had hardened. 'I told you,' he said abruptly, 'I had all sorts of jobs, anything I could find. Once I had ambitions to be a professional actor, but . . . ' He glanced at his watch. 'Oh, just look at the time! We must get back.' He started scrambling to his feet and his expression was inscrutable. As he began striding down the hill I had to struggle to keep up with him. Well, I had touched on a raw nerve there and wondered what the story behind that could be.

We were back in the village when Alexis who must have seen us approaching, came running out of the pub with an air of urgency about her. 'Oh, Bron — there you are — at last! We've been looking all over for you. Where've you been?' Not waiting for a reply she went on, 'Becca's had a bit of an accident.'

'What?' Bron followed her inside and I trailed after them. 'What kind of accident?' he demanded.

'Well, it's not really serious,' Alexis said, 'but . . . come and see for yourself — she's over here.' She grabbed his arm and pulled him across the room.

Rebecca, looking pale and shaken, was sitting in the corner of the bar on a worn leather banquette, while the landlady, a plump and motherly woman, was hovering beside her with a box of tissues in her hand. As we drew nearer, she bent to dab one gently at the corner of the girl's mouth before handing it to her, and was making soothing noises as Rebecca caught sight of Bron and began to sob.

'Whatever's happened to you?' he asked, and all the colour drained from his face as he sat down at her side and took one of her hands in his. 'Oh, B-Bron!' she wailed and laid her head against his shoulder. 'I tripped and smashed my face against the corner of the counter,' her voice came thick and muffled, 'and now, look!'

Rebecca removed the tissue she had been holding to her face and Bron drew back and sucked in his breath with a whistle of sympathy. 'Whew — that looks painful, let me see it properly.' He tipped up her chin and peered closely.

From where I was standing just beside them, I could see how bruised and swollen her face was. One cheek was scratched and streaked with blood, and a huge bruise was beginning to spread from her nose to the side of her mouth. 'I bit my tongue too as I fell,' she went on with difficulty. The landlady who had gone behind the bar to draw a glass of water, now returned to her side and Rebecca sipped at it gratefully, wincing at the discomfort.

'Oh, poor Rebecca!' I remarked to Alexis, 'what a horrible thing to happen.' She nodded and murmured softly, 'But just look at the shoes she's wearing — was it any wonder she tripped?'

I did, and felt my eyes widen as I understood. Backless straw mules with four-inch heels. Coming down the steps into the dimness of the bar, blinded from the bright sunshine outside . . . it didn't need much imagination to picture the scene.

'And I twisted my ankle too,' Rebecca wailed, and fingered it with her free hand. Bron was obviously thinking the same as we were, as he gave a snort and glanced at the discarded shoes. 'I'm not surprised,' he said shortly, and added, 'As soon as you feel able to move, I'll get someone to take you over to the first-aid van and get it strapped up, and have something put on that face as well. Then I suggest you stay there and lie down for an hour or two, Becca. Recover from the shock. OK?'

Bron's tone of voice was now verging on the brisk and I knew from what he had told me earlier about his tight work schedule, that he was itching to get on with the filming. I also recalled what he had said about me coaching Rebecca in her Cornish accent, but of course there was no chance of that now. Poor Bron — he wouldn't get the first scene finished today after all.

Soon Rebecca, carrying the fateful shoes, was being led limping away by Sam and Isabel's mother, who had promised to look after her. Barefoot, she looked so much smaller that she seemed to have actually shrunk and now resembled even more the old woman she'd been playing. Then I could almost hear Bron's sigh of relief as he clapped his hands and called out, 'ready everybody — back to work.'

But I was totally unprepared for his next remark. As we all drifted outside, he laid a hand on my arm to draw me away from the others and said, 'Vicky, you know you agreed to help Becca with her speech this afternoon?'

I nodded. 'Yes, I was just thinking it's a pity you won't be able to finish that scene today after all.'

'Oh, but I intend to,' came the reply,

'with a little help from you.' I looked up in astonishment at his determined expression and penetrating gaze. 'M — me?' I faltered.

'Vicky, you watched that scene over and over again this morning — you must know the words off by heart by now.' His searching gaze held mine and I felt my heart sink as I finally twigged. 'You don't mean . . .' I clapped a hand to my mouth. 'Bron — I couldn't!'

'Of course you could!' he gave my arm a shake. 'You can do it perfectly — much better than Becca ever could. Vicky, I need you — please don't let me down.' The grip on my arm tightened a fraction and as we looked into each other's eyes I felt a flicker of something, a new awareness perhaps, pass between us.

So how could I resist the pleading in that brilliant blue gaze when every nerve-ending was being stretched to breaking-point, and my legs were turning to jelly? From stage-fright of course.

# 3

Still quaking, I enveloped myself in Rebecca's cloak, drew the two children to my side and took her place on the hummock. Bron was quite right — I did know the dialogue, and once we'd started I began to feel less nervous. It was quite fun relapsing into the broad Cornish dialect which I'd been brought up with, but which had been frowned upon at school because it was considered 'common' to speak that way. I became more and more absorbed in my part, until I was almost unaware of the eye of the camera and of Andy crouching behind me with the 'sausage'.

' . . . he was the most handsome man in the village and for miles around . . . ' I said, remembering to raise my hand in a sweep of the scenery and at the same moment met Bron's eyes, which were focused intently on me. Realising what I had just said, my voice faltered for a split second, but hastily recovered as I reminded myself of the importance of this scene. I had been entrusted with a professional role here and I must act like a pro. I tore my gaze away from Bron and back to the children as I went on, 'More than that, he could sing . . . ' and turned my full attention to the part.

My heart was in my mouth as I came to the end of my speech and a brief silence fell. Then I shook myself free of the hood and raised my head to see Bron striding towards me with a huge smile across his face. 'Bravo, Vicky, that was brilliant! Your voice was perfect, and you even remembered the right gestures. Well done!' He stopped beside us and ran a hand through his hair. 'I can't tell you how grateful I am to you for stepping in like that.'

I let out all the breath I hadn't realised I'd been holding and rose to my feet. 'Oh, I'm so glad it was OK,' I replied. 'Actually I quite enjoyed doing it — after I stopped being nervous, that is.'

'Have you ever done any acting?' Bron enquired as we fell into step and made our way over the grass towards the refreshment table. I shook my head. 'Not really. I was in the school Dramatic Society, but that's all.' I accepted the cup of tea he handed me and we sat down on one of the flat rocks bordering the road. 'I've always enjoyed live theatre,' I went on, 'but until recently there wasn't much down this way. Now we have the Hall for Cornwall — that's in Truro — which was opened a few years ago and we get more professional productions coming. I do go there sometimes — and of course there's the open air theatre at Porthcurno during the summer season — the Minack. Have you ever been there, Bron?'

'No,' he shook his head, 'but I'd like to. I've heard it's in a fabulous setting, overlooking the sea and kind of built out of the natural cliffs, is that right?'

I nodded. 'Absolutely.'

He paused and half-turned towards me. As our eyes met he added, 'Maybe we could go one evening. Would you like to?'

I almost choked on a mouthful of tea. Just us — would I like to! I felt my eyes sparkling and tried to control the delight that must have been written all over my face. 'I'd love to,' I replied as soberly as I was able. 'I'll get hold of a programme and we can see what's on.'

★　★　★

I walked on air for the rest of the day, even when I was sitting right at the back of the church watching the second scene, well out of the range of the camera, I couldn't stop thinking about it.

The 'congregation', made up as Bron had said, of the local people brought in as extras were all clad in Victorian dress which had been stored in one of the enormous trailers I had seen up by the farm and fitted by the dedicated wardrobe team.

It amused me to see that Alexis, as the mermaid in disguise, was wearing a a trailing gown of sea-green, topped by a sleek coat of sealskin with a matching hat. A nice touch on somebody's part, I thought, and said as much as we rose to leave the church and I bumped into Bron coming up the aisle. He grinned widely and replied, 'Och, that was my idea as a matter of fact.'

I raised an eyebrow in surprise. 'Oh?' We began to shuffle towards the door, caught up in the press of people.

'Yes, it came to me because of a legend we have back home.' Bron put a hand under my elbow to steer me around a pillar — I'd been so intent on listening to him that I would have walked right into it. My whole arm tingled with a jolt like an electric shock, but he gave no sign of being aware of it, as he went on. 'We have legends about mermaids on Orkney as well, you know,' his eyes twinkled, 'but up there we call them 'Selkies'.'

'Really?' He had my interest now.

'Aye. And they can assume human guise as well — just like your Zennor mermaid.' Bron was still holding on to my arm although the danger was over, and we were walking down the aisle together like a couple . . . and just as if . . .

I swallowed and took a deep breath as I made myself concentrate on his story. 'But,' he was saying now, 'a selkie if it loses its coat, is condemned to stay in the world of humans forever and never go back to the sea.'

'Oh, right,' I smiled as we reached the entrance and he withdrew his hand from my arm, which felt suddenly chilled even as we stepped out into the warm sunshine.

It was then that I noticed Rebecca hovering on the doorstep. 'Hi, Becca,' Bron stopped at her side. 'How are you feeling now? Shouldn't you be resting that ankle?'

She scowled. 'It's much better

actually since it's been bandaged, and I've been resting all the afternoon. I shall be quite all right for work again tomorrow.'

'Ah,' Bron paused and nibbled his lip. 'Well, as a matter of fact, we did finish shooting your scene today. Vicky did a splendid job with the Cornish voice and it went well.' Obviously noticing the expression on her face he hastily added, 'I've another part lined up for you, Becky,' Bron laid a hand on her arm as he added, 'I thought when Matty goes off with the mermaid you could play his abandoned girl-friend.'

'But that's not a speaking part!' Rebecca's eyes flashed in anger.

'Exactly,' Bron muttered.

'And she only appears for a minute — right at the end.' Her indignant voice carried and several people glanced curiously at the two as they passed.

Bron's features hardened and he shrugged uncomfortably. 'You will of course, be paid at the same rate.'

'But Bron . . . ' she pleaded,

clutching at the hand on her arm and keeping it there as I tried to extricate myself from the scene.

'Bye, Bron,' I said quickly, 'I'll see you tomorrow,' and turned to go, as Rebecca continued to hold on to him.

'Surely,' she said and her cold eyes raked me up and down, 'you must surely have plenty of your own work to do, haven't you?'

'Ah, but Vicky told me she's between jobs at the moment,' Bron interrupted and smiled at me. 'That right, Vicky?' I nodded a reply. 'You are you coming over again tomorrow, then?' Bron gave me a searching look.

I turned to him with a smile. 'I expect so — I'd love to see the rest of the filming. And I'll bring the programme for the Minack — I know Diane will have some in the shop.'

'Great, I'll see you then,' Bron turned away with a wave, and I felt Rebecca's chilly gaze on me as she looked over her shoulder before following him. Her obvious dislike of me, and yes, jealousy, was plain to see in the look, which would have cut glass.

* * *

'Diane,' I said later that evening, 'have you got any programmes for the Minack downstairs in the shop?' My sister looked up from the book in which she had been absorbed, and pushed a strand of hair back over one ear. Looking at me over the top of her spectacles she said, 'Yes, I'm pretty sure we have. Why — are you thinking of going?'

'Oh — um — yes.' I kept my voice casual. 'Bron suggested we might — he's never been there of course.'

Diane's brows rose a fraction. 'Oh, so you're going out together, are you?' She kept her attention on me, obviously waiting for a confidence.

She seemed disappointed when I said airily, 'Oh, I just thought he ought to see one of the beauty spots of Cornwall before he goes back.' I turned away, took the key of the shop from its hook and went clattering down the stairs before she could ask any further questions.

*   *   *

'Haven't they finished that filming yet?' Diane asked when I told her next morning that I was going back to Zennor.

'Oh, no, you'd never believe how long it takes to get even one small scene perfect. It took them most of yesterday to get the first part right, because the girl who's narrating the story couldn't speak with a Cornish accent.'

I was on the verge of telling her how I'd taken over the part, when she broke in. 'But haven't you got your own work to do, Vicky?' she remarked, quite innocently echoing Rebecca's remark of yesterday. 'Can you afford to take all this time off?' Heat flooded my face and the moment was lost as I felt a flash of irritation.

Trying hard not to snap at her I replied, 'I've finished all the shots for the calendar, Di. And in any case, it's not 'all this time' — only a few days. Surely I'm entitled to that much without criticism?'

Her eyes widened and she held up a placating hand. 'Sorr — ee, sorry. Of course you are. Have a nice day,' she added hastily, calling to my retreating back. I waved without turning my head and set off.

\* \* \*

'Right everybody, I'm hoping to cover scene three today,' I heard Bron announcing as I drove into the car park. The crew were gathered outside the back-packers' hostel and he was perched on top of one of the big rocks marking the boundary. 'Especially as the weather is set to change — they're forecasting rain coming in this evening, so let's get on with it. You all know your places.'

He jumped down and raised a hand to me. 'Hi, Vicky, all right?'

I smiled, as I replied, 'Fine,' and wandered over towards them all. Then I was shaken rigid as Bron said, 'You do know you're in this scene as well, don't you?'

'Me?' I felt colour flood my face and rise to the roots of my hair. 'N — no, I didn't. I had no idea.'

Bron's jaw dropped and he seemed as astonished as I was. 'But I thought I'd told you — oh, sorry, Vicky.' He ran a hand through his hair, already tousled by the breeze that was steadily strengthening from the west. 'Yes, the old woman is in this last scene too, but she doesn't speak.' He pointed towards the hillock on which we'd sat the previous day.

'She stands with the children, looking seawards and pointing towards the path where the mermaid is leading Matty away from the village. They go hand in hand towards the stream that runs into the sea, then enter the water, while the village folk watch from the sidelines and some of them cluster around Matty's abandoned girlfriend and try to comfort her.'

That's Rebecca, I thought as Bron went on, 'She's broken-hearted and weeping piteously, holding out imploring hands in vain as the couple get smaller and smaller until they vanish into the distance. There's a passage of background music here, and the last shot of all is a close-up of the stream meeting the sea, then the camera pans in on the breaking surf.'

I could imagine that, the white water streaming off the waves as the wind blew back their crests into the flying spray that children called 'white horses'. It would make a powerful scene.

'That's fantastic, Bron,' I said and meant it, looking at him with a new respect. For there was far more to this man than met the eye. Imaginative, creative and with a sensitivity I had not come across before in the male sex. And as deep as the ocean itself when it came to giving any of his inner self away. I knew no more about him now than when we'd first met.

I was aware of a few glowering looks from Rebecca, who I thought, overacted her part and milked it for all she was worth, but she didn't speak a word to me for the day. Not that I cared particularly, but her attitude cast a small cloud over my enjoyment of the play-acting. I didn't like falling out with anyone, especially when it wasn't any fault of mine. However, the scene had gone well and Bron seemed pleased with the day's work.

'Thanks everybody,' he called. 'Tomorrow I hope, we can get the editing done and have a trial viewing of the whole thing. I've already got a few stills we can look at first while that's being done. So — see you here in the morning at the usual time.'

We exchanged a few words as we were packing up, and just before I left, Bron came across as I was getting into my car and propped an elbow on the open door.

'By the way, Vicky,' he said casually, 'Did you get hold of a programme for the Minack?' My spirits lifted. I hadn't been prepared to bring up the subject again unless he did, in case it looked as if I was too eager. But now I nodded and pulling the leaflet from the glove compartment, I handed it to him. 'Do you like Shakespeare, Bron?' I enquired as he started riffling through it. 'They're doing *A Midsummer Night's Dream*, this week. A professional touring company — they're usually very good.'

Bron raised his eyes and gave me a heart-stopping smile. 'Ah, Shakespeare — oh, yes.' Suddenly he straightened up, struck a pose and declared, 'Ill-met by moonlight, proud Titania'.'

'You know it!' I gave a squeal of delight as I squinted up at him, the sun in my eyes. Then as I raised a hand to shade them, something clicked in my mind. 'Bron,' I said, abruptly changing the subject. 'Is your name short for something? I've been meaning to ask you.' A look of discomfort replaced the smile and he turned away. 'Yes, but I never let anybody know what it is,' he said, turning back to me with a glare and scuffing a toe in the gravel.

I gave a gleeful chuckle and said with mischief, 'It's Oberon, isn't it?'

Bron paused then turned back to me, colouring, and nodded. 'I'm afraid so,' he added with a rueful smile. 'So you guessed.' He spread his hands wide and shrugged. 'King of the fairies, I ask you! Are you surprised I keep it a secret?'

'Oh dear!' I burst out laughing and covered my mouth with a hand as I gripped the steering wheel with the other. 'I do understand, Bron, really,' I added weakly, as I tried to be serious. 'But it is funny.'

'Promise you won't breathe a word, Vicky,' Bron said with a note of pleading in his voice as he bent and clutched at my arm. 'Nobody on the set knows and they haven't asked.' He drew away and ran agitated fingers through his hair, leaving it standing on end.

'Of course I won't, I would never betray a secret,' I said, slightly indignant, as Bron gave a sigh of apparent relief.

'Sorry, I didn't really think for a minute you would.'

He turned his attention back to the theatre programme he was still holding and glanced through the details. 'OK. I'll get this organised before we all break up — see how many people will want to come, and whether Andy's willing to drive the minibus, for a start.'

I hardly heard the rest of it, the blood was singing so loudly in my ears, and I felt suddenly chilled to the bone. He meant to take the whole company! Oh, Bron, I cried inwardly, and I thought we were going to have a magical night out together, just the two of us. How could I have been so mistaken!

But thinking back, Bron had said nothing to indicate that he had meant just the two of us. It had been all my own fault for jumping to conclusions, because it was what I wanted to happen.

Then some of what he was saying began to penetrate, as I realised he had asked me a question. 'Maybe we can have a barbie on the beach and a swim — make a real break of it — a kind of celebration at finishing the film. That'd be good, wouldn't it? What do you think?' He turned bright eyes full of enthusiasm on me. I nodded woodenly as I pasted a smile to my face. Then I tilted my chin and, swallowing my disappointment before he could see it, I forced my voice to sound natural as I murmured some agreeable reply.

⋆　⋆　⋆

'You're not in the best of moods this evening, are you?' Diane remarked mildly, as I arrived home and flung my bag in a corner with a muttered greeting, before stomping downstairs again.

'You look as if you'd lost a pound

and found a penny,' she added, sliding a plate of delicious looking food in front of me. 'Something wrong, is there?'

It might as well have been dry bread as pork stir-fry for all the appetite I had. I grunted and picked up my fork. 'I'm OK. Just tired.'

She slipped into her seat opposite and regarded me solemnly. 'Not sickening for something, are you? There's a bout of summer flu going around, so Mrs. Laity was saying.'

'Oh, leave it out, Di, I'm perfectly all right, I told you,' I snapped. 'There's no need to fuss like a mother hen.' Then I caught sight of her hurt expression and relented. 'I'm sorry — I didn't mean to yell at you. But I am perfectly all right, really.' I waved my fork for emphasis. 'No hassle, no problems.' I forced myself to smile brightly and the worry lines vanished as she relaxed.

I was thinking at the back of my mind how good it would be in many ways to have a place of my own, with no watchful eyes witnessing my every move, then felt a stab of the familiar guilt and heaved a sigh. Was I ever going to be able to broach the subject to Diane? Because until I found out whether she genuinely liked having me around for company — and for my contribution to the housekeeping money — I could hardly do so. But it was such a delicate matter — and of course she would tell me to do what I wanted, keeping her own feelings to herself, for my sister was the most unselfish person I knew. But at this rate we would still be living together when we were both old and grey.

Next morning the sky was overcast and threatening rain, with a chilly south-westerly wind edging in through the bedroom window. Not a day for shorts and tee-shirt I thought, glancing over towards the Mount which was partially obscured by a veil of pearly cloud. The sea was a dull pewter colour, sullenly slapping at the shore in fitful bursts of spray, and did nothing to cheer my spirits. As I turned away and reached for jeans and a sweater, a sudden flurry of rain hit the glass and I peered out in the misty greyness again.

Great banks of cloud were swirling in over the water and the Mount had completely vanished. I felt a stab of annoyance, for this was no day to be going to Zennor. For one thing the coast road would make for dangerous driving in fog like this, and for another, the crew would be indoors, crammed into the tents and trailers, and I had no desire to be cooped up in such close quarters with Rebecca. No, I would make the most of the morning here instead, doing my share of the household chores and sorting out my own work. Perhaps the weather would blow over later.

I had slept later than usual and Diane was already busy in the shop when I hauled out the cleaner and prepared to tackle the bedrooms. As I got down to it I realised that mine was like a tip, and felt a stab of guilt over the time I'd been spending at Zennor recently. Especially as Diane's room in contrast was impeccably neat and tidy. Just like my sister, I thought as I pushed the cleaner over the carpet, she never gives anything of herself away — no wonder it was so hard to question her about her feelings.

I was surprised to find it was approaching lunchtime by the time I had sorted everything and brought some kind of order to my room, and I'd been so engrossed that I hadn't glanced outside at all. Now as I crossed to the window to shake out the duster I could hardly believe my eyes. The few ragged remains of clouds which were left were rapidly drifting away out to sea and the sun, getting stronger by the minute, was peering benignly down from a patch of unbelievably blue sky. My spirits immediately lifted like the weather and as I stowed the cleaning things back into their cupboard I could not suppress a smile of satisfaction.

It was at that moment I heard a voice

calling my name from the bottom of the stairwell, and going to the door I had the shock of my life, for there was Bron, taking the steps two at a time on his way up to the flat.

# 4

My heart had started pounding so loudly I felt sure it must be obvious to him, and the shock had set my legs shaking so that I had to clutch the doorframe for support.

'Bron!' I goggled at him like a fool. 'What are you doing here?'

He joined me on the landing and grinned. 'Hi Vicky,' he flattened his rumpled hair with one hand, 'I know this must be a bit of a shock, but I couldn't find your phone number in a hurry.' He raised a brow as he added, 'Can I come in?'

I shook myself back to life and jumped to one side, feeling more foolish than ever as I gestured him through the doorway. 'Oh — oh, yes, of course. I'm so sorry — in here,' I stammered as I led the way into the sitting room. 'The phone's under the name of the shop,' I explained, sinking into an armchair and waving him towards its twin, 'So how did you find me?'

'Simple.' He crossed his long jeans-clad legs and leant back. 'I checked out the second-hand bookshops in the town — and found there was only one. So here I am. I had a word with your sister on the way in and she told me to come right up.'

'Oh, I see.' Tongue-tied, I could only stare at him. To ask outright what he wanted and why he had come would hardly seem friendly. 'Er — would you like a cup of coffee — or something?' I asked into the small silence that had fallen. 'Oh, no — no thanks.' Bron shook his head. 'I can't stop. I only came to tell you that if we want to go to the Minack, it'll have to be this evening. They're booked up for all the rest of the week and they can't take so many of us, except for tonight.' He spread his hands apologetically. 'I'm sorry to spring it on you like this, Vicky — and I do hope you can make it at such short notice,' he said with concern, 'but I had to take what they offered, it was that or nothing.'

A small voice in my head was whispering, so much for throwing it open to everyone then — if it had just been the two of us, there would be no problem ... But Bron had after all, come haring over here especially to explain, so perhaps he did care, a bit. Or maybe he just felt obligated because it had been my idea in the first place. That would be more like it, I thought darkly, and gave a sigh for what might have been.

But he was waiting for my reply. 'Well, I did have other plans,' I lied, crossing my fingers and keeping my voice cool, 'but I suppose I can put those on hold. So yes, I'll come. As there seems to be no alternative.' I regarded him with a level stare.

But he did seem genuinely pleased, as his face brightened and lost its anxious look. 'Oh, I'm so glad — it wouldn't be the same without you,' he said with a smile. So what was I to make of that? I gave a mental shrug. But I felt my whole body relaxing in the warmth of that smile and my resentment melting away like frost in the sun.

'So what are the arrangements?' I asked, turning away as I straightened a cushion and became brisk and business-like. Bron leaned forward and rested his arms on his knees. 'I thought — if you don't mind doubling back a few miles, Vicky — you could come across and leave your car in Zennor, so we can all go to Porthcurno in the minibus.' He quirked an eyebrow and I nodded my agreement. 'If you can get over as soon as you can after lunch, we'll get down there say mid-afternoon, and we can have a swim or relax on the beach, then cook a barbie before the performance. That OK with you?'

Bron stood up and uncurled his lean figure from the depths of the chair. 'OK, lovely,' I replied absently, as thinking aloud I added, 'I'd better get some things together and find some food to bring. I'll have to raid the freezer and see if we've got any sausages left.' I rose to my feet as well and he made his way towards the door. 'So how did the work go this morning, Bron?'

His expression darkened. 'Oh, not too well actually. Someone made a cock-up of the editing, and I wanted to do a retake of some of the last scene, but of course the weather didn't allow for that, and now I'm running behind schedule. But,' he waved a hand to indicate the bright sunlight now streaming in over the bay, 'perhaps we'll be luckier tomorrow.'

'Oh, I hope so.' We'd reached the top of the stairs when I said, 'Thanks for coming over, Bron, I appreciate it.' He raised a hand dismissively as he went clattering down the steps.

'No problem,' he called over his shoulder. 'See you later.'

★   ★   ★

78

The weather had lived up to its promise and we set off in almost a holiday mood, with everyone looking forward to a break from work. I'd just taken a window-seat when to my surprise Bron came up through the bus and sat beside me. He was closely followed by Rebecca, who by her thunderous expression had obviously been hoping they would share, but she sat as near to him as she could, across the aisle in the outside seat beside Alex.

Bron and I chatted about nothing in particular for a while, until I realised this was a perfect opportunity to find out a bit more about him, so I deliberately started fishing. The conversation had turned to the play we would be seeing later, and the company which was performing, so I said quite innocently, 'Bron, didn't you tell me that you wanted to be a professional actor once?' Abruptly he turned his head away and his face darkened. 'What happened to stop you?'

Looking down at his hands which

were clasped in his lap he replied with a shrug, 'Och, it's a long story, Vicky, you wouldn't be interested.'

I refused to accept the obvious brush-off, replying, 'Oh, but I would, very much.'

Bron's shoulders lifted in a sigh as he seemed to realise that I had him cornered and he couldn't get up and walk away, as I knew he wanted to, so he turned back and gave me a level stare. 'Oh, all right then. Well, it was like this.' He gazed past me at the moving scenery outside and took a breath.

'I don't know if I told you I come from a big family,' he began.

'No, you didn't.' I shook my head.

'Oh, well, yes, I have twin brothers and two sisters, all younger than me.' My eyebrows rose as I wondered if they were all as gorgeous-looking as him.

'Mm, I see what you mean.'

Bron shifted and stretched his legs out into the aisle. 'We lived on a farm — not huge, more of a croft really. But

Dad kept sheep and a few cattle, and grew all our own vegetables. It overlooked the sea — there were plenty of fish for the taking — and it was quite an idyllic life for us children. Although we all had to pitch in and work after school and at weekends. Out in all winds and weathers, but we never caught as much as a cold. Mum used to spin and card our wool, and knit jumpers for us all, as well as to sell to the summer visitors. Nobody was ever idle.'

I didn't say a word in case I interrupted Bron's train of thought. Now that he had begun to talk, he seemed to be reliving the past as if he'd forgotten I was there.

'Then when I was sixteen, my father had an accident.' His brow furrowed and he looked down at his clasped hands as he paused for a moment. 'He'd borrowed a bull to put with our cows, but something must have spooked the animal, because it suddenly turned nasty and came at him.'

I sucked in a breath, totally absorbed

in the story. 'Well, Dad took to his heels and ran, but he wasn't fast enough. I was there, Vicky,' his mouth twisted. 'I saw it all and couldn't do anything to help because it all happened so fast. The bull tossed Dad into the air — I can see it as if it was yesterday,' his voice quivered, 'and he landed in the hedge. He cracked his head on a stone, and it left him blinded. He lost his sight completely, almost overnight.' Bron turned to meet my horrified gaze and spread his hands wide.

'So what could I do?' He shrugged at the hopelessness of it all. 'I couldn't leave home after that — I was the eldest son, indispensable to my mother and the younger children. I did my best to take my father's place but it was hard, very hard.' Bron's eyes had misted and with a sigh he was back in the past again.

'After a while my father learnt to live with his disability — he had tremendous courage and willpower — and he still managed to do certain jobs around the farm. But we were only a handful of children, we just couldn't cope. He couldn't afford hired help and the farm became more and more rundown until we had to sell up and move into a small, cramped cottage.

'Of course as the younger ones grew up and went to work, things became easier and we moved eventually into a comfortable house in Stromness, where my parents still live. Then at last I was able to leave home. But,' he turned to me with pain in his eyes, 'I was too old by that time to train as an actor — or for any career really. So I went from casual job to anything I could get, and did some amateur filming in a club that I joined. And now, here I am, on the first fulfilling assignment I've ever had. So you can see how important it is to me.'

He paused and sighed deeply. 'So there you are, Vicky. I hope I haven't bored you rigid with it all.'

It was all I could do to stop myself reaching out to squeeze his hand. It lay so close to mine and the expression on his face was so desolate that I longed to offer comfort. But I kept my fingers clasped tightly in my lap and said softly, 'Thanks for telling me, Bron. I'm really sorry for the way things turned out.'

He raised a shoulder. 'That's life,' he said giving me a rueful smile. 'It has a habit of smacking you in the mouth if you get too ambitious. But look!' he peered past me through the window, 'I think we must be nearly there. Oh, wow — what a view! Is this it?'

I jerked back to the present and followed Bron's gaze. The minibus was negotiating a series of white-knuckle hairpin bends as the road descended into Porthcurno, and below us lay an expanse of clean white sand and turquoise water that could have come straight from an advertisement for a Mediterranean holiday.

We all scrambled out and gathered up our belongings before trooping down to the beach. The cove was almost deserted, apart from a family building sandcastles on the far side, and a woman walking her dog along the edge of the sea. Behind us sheer granite cliffs rose to the skyline, and stopping to turn back and look upwards I pointed out the Minack theatre carefully hewn out of the natural rock, its outline kept low and cleverly designed to be as unobtrusive as possible.

'What a spectacular place!' 'Look at the colour of that sea!' 'I'm going for a swim right away.' 'I'm going to lie down and soak up this sun.' Shouts and squeals of delight echoed around the cove as the company split up and went their preferred ways. I wandered across to a sheltered nook between two rocks which were warm to the touch where they had been baking in the full sun, and put down my things. Then I took the food out before it began to cook where it was, and placed that in a cooler place behind the rocks, on some damp sand.

'Coming for a dip, Vicky?' I looked up to see Bron towering over me, already changed into swimming trunks, with a towel slung around his neck. The breath caught in my throat and my heart turned a somersault at the sheer virility of this man. Unclothed, the whole of his lean and perfect figure gleamed golden in the clear light, from the finely chiselled features of his face to the broad shoulders, slim hips, and long, long legs. Outlined against the sun Bron was the image of every famous statue I'd ever seen.

'Oh — er — no, I don't think so, thanks.' Instinct told me that he would be a superb swimmer while I, despite loving the water, was terrified of being out of my depth and preferred to splash about in the waves within reach of dry land. And I had no desire to show myself up in any company, least of all Bron's. 'I'm going to sunbathe for a bit,' I smiled as I spread my towel and reached for the sunblock. 'Maybe later.'

'OK,' Bron said, and was turning to go, when he caught sight of the bottle and held out a hand, 'shall I do your back before I go?' he asked casually. So stunned was I that I almost upset the whole lot, but I managed to stutter, 'Oh — um — all right. Thanks.' He knelt down and leaned over me as if it was the most natural thing in the world, and when his warm palms began to stroke my back, gently but insistently, my insides dissolved into jelly and it was as much as I could do to stop myself from turning and throwing my arms around his neck.

I bit down hard on my bottom lip to control the pounding in my blood and wished the moment could last forever.

'I used to do this a lot for my sister when we were all at home,' Bron remarked.

Striving to keep the atmosphere light, I joked, 'Oh, so that's where you learned your sureness of touch — I thought it wasn't the first time you've done it.'

'Bron — do my back as well, will you, darling?' chimed in another voice.

I raised my head, squinting against the sun, and there was Rebecca standing over us, wearing the scantiest bikini I'd ever seen, with a pair of sunglasses pushed up into her hair and carrying a beach towel, which she proceeded to spread out beside mine.

Bron stood up and wiped his hands down the side of his trunks. 'Sorry Becca, I'm just going for a swim. I expect Vicky will oblige if you ask her. See you both later.' He raised a hand and began to lope away over the sand. Rebecca's expression was thunderous as picking up the towel, she stalked off without a word to me, and stretched herself full length on the sand a few yards away.

When the swimmers returned, someone organised a game of volleyball with much shouting and laughter, and soon it was time for the barbecue. 'Alex,' I said as I found myself sitting beside her, both of us nibbling on chicken drumsticks, and I was watching Bron and Rebecca sitting very close together, both of them laughing uproariously at some private joke, 'I've been wondering about this for ages — are Bron and Becca a pair, or not?'

'Oh — um — ' Alex followed my gaze and lifted her shoulders. 'I'm not sure really. I think Becca would like them to be, but as for Bron — he's pretty much his own man. I don't think he wants any attachments at the moment,' she added shrewdly, tossing her chicken bone into the waste bag and wiping her fingers on a paper napkin. Narrowing her eyes she looked intently at the two. 'This job is very important to him and I think he wants to give it his all, without any distractions.'

I nodded. 'That was the impression I had as well.' My gaze rested on the couple, who with some others were now packing up the left-over food and stamping out the fire. So, I sighed, I was none the wiser and likely to remain so.

★　★　★

Soon we were climbing the steep track up to the theatre and looking for our seats on the grassy terracing above the stage. Out over the water, the sun was making a shimmering pathway of molten gold as it began its slow descent towards the horizon, and the sky was washed with streaks of lemon and powder pink. The quiet waves of the summer sea plashed gently below while Shakespeare's Oberon told how ' . . . once I sat upon a promontory, and heard a mermaid . . . uttering her . . . song . . . and certain stars shot madly from their spheres to hear the sea-maid's music.' I glanced towards Bron but he was studying his programme and had obviously not noticed the allusion as I had.

From where I was sitting, the scent of honeysuckle and thyme wafted on the cooling air, while bees were buzzing lazily in the cream cups of tiny burnet roses on the bank above us. I noticed a cluster of tiny wild violas with their delicate pansy-like faces, and smiled as the lines from the play ran through my head, reminding me of Shakespeare's love-potion ' . . . a little western flower . . . maidens call it Love-in-Idleness'.

And down on the stage, Oberon the fairy king was now reciting the lines that could have been written for this night. 'I know a bank whereon the wild thyme blows — where oxlip and the nodding violet grows — quite over-canopied with lush woodbine, with sweet musk-roses and with eglantine . . .'

Nothing could have been more apt. It was a perfect, magical moment and instinctively I sought out Bron again where he was sitting further along the row. As our eyes met and I knew he had been looking for me at the same moment, my throat contracted and I felt the sting of sudden tears as I turned my head quickly away. 'The course of true love never did run smooth', as Lysander had lamented earlier. More fitting words were never spoken, and I gave a mental shrug. Him and me both,

I thought with a sigh, two victims of 'Love-in-Idleness' — unrequited love. For yes, I loved this man, loved him completely and unconditionally, forever. But that was my own private problem and I would have to learn to live with it. I bit my lip and forced my attention back to the stage.

★ ★ ★

It was a more subdued party who filed down the hill to the mini-bus at the end of the show, as if the fairytale magic of the play still held us in thrall. By now a half-moon had risen and was throwing a cascade of silver light over the landscape. As each boulder and building became etched in sharp relief and the shadows beneath subtly darkened, the scene bore no resemblance to the sun-soaked panorama of the afternoon. With the velvet canopy of the night sky studded with a million stars, it was awesome and we could well have been still spellbound in an imaginary world.

I almost fell asleep on the bus, worn out by the after-effect of sea and sun, combined with heightened emotions and the lateness of the hour, and was aroused with a start as we drove into the Zennor car park and pulled up with a jerk.

'Oh, Vicky,' said Bron as he passed me in the aisle while I was still getting myself together, 'Don't forget I'll need you tomorrow for the retake of scene three, will you?'

'OK,' I replied, looking at my watch. 'It is almost tomorrow, actually,' I replied laughing. 'Perhaps I won't bother to go home — I could sleep in the car, I suppose!' I joked.

'Oh, you needn't make it very early,' Bron called over his shoulder as he was pushed forwards by the crowd coming behind him, 'have a bit of a lie-in if you like — I expect we all will.'

★　★　★

And after tossing and turning for what seemed like hours, while the scenes from the play did a re-run like a video behind my eyes, and I couldn't get Bron's image out of my mind either, I did sleep much later than usual. Hoping I wasn't going to find that the whole company was held up waiting for me, I drove dangerously fast along the treacherous coast road, with my heart in my mouth and my foot covering the brake pedal, ready to slam it down hard if anything came at me round the hidden bends. But all was well and I slewed into the car park and pulled up in a skitter of gravel just as they were all taking their places.

'Ah, Vicky, there you are!' Bron waved with the clip-board he was holding, as a voice at my elbow muttered, 'At last.' I didn't need to turn round to know who it was behind me.

The words hung in the air about us as Bron indicated that I should join the children on the hill, ready to start.

It all seemed to me to go really well,

and the ending was quite touching as I heard the musical backing for the first time. Played on recorders by the local schoolchildren, the tune was ethereal, haunting and repetitive, rising and falling like the waves of the sea, and perfectly complemented the acting. As the mermaid led her lover into the water and they disappeared forever, I actually felt a lump in my throat. If only fairytale endings happened in real life!

As we dispersed for the mid-morning break, Bron caught me up and we walked together towards to the refreshment area. 'I'm really sorry I was so late this morning, Bron,' I said with a small smile, 'I'm afraid I did oversleep. I hope I didn't hold you up too much in the event.'

'Er — no, no, of course not,' he said hastily. Too hastily to be entirely true, I thought with embarrassment, and glanced away to encounter a glare from Rebecca. Oh why couldn't she get off my back, I thought crossly, feeling my face flush.

'Oh, Vicky,' Bron was saying, 'I told the others earlier, before you got here, that I've put out a spread of the stills we took yesterday. If you want to take a look, they're just inside the door of the pub.'

'Mm, right, I will.' I was just drawing breath to ask Bron if he had enjoyed the play, but someone else had claimed his attention and he was heading off elsewhere. I shrugged, helped myself to a coffee and took it with me into the pub. The photographs were laid out on a trestle table just inside the door and I paused to let my eyes adjust after the brightness outside. Then feeling a need to visit the loo, I placed my cup carefully down and went upstairs.

When I came back again, all hell had broken loose. It took me a minute to see what was going on, and when I did, my legs turned instantly to jelly and I had to clutch at the newel post for support.

Hot coffee was pouring all over the table, the photos and the floor. Rebecca and Alex were frantically dabbing at the flood with paper napkins and as I stood transfixed, Bron suddenly arrived on the scene.

'What on earth . . . ?' he began, 'Oh, no!' Then with a howl of rage as he realised what had happened, he roared, 'What stupid, bloody idiot's responsible for this?'

Rebecca raised her head but continued to scrub at the photos. 'Well, I'm not one for telling tales, Bron, as you know, but Vicky left her coffee here you see, and the table's a bit rocky.' She raised demure eyes to Bron's furious face and slowly shook her head. 'But I'm sure she didn't know that. It was just a horrible accident.'

With a sly look she turned in my direction, and the malice in her eyes chilled me as, unseen by the others, she gave a small, triumphant smile.

# 5

All eyes were upon me, practically the whole cast was there, staring transfixed at the scene. Even Sam and Isabel the children, were looking at me with big round eyes as they held tight to their mother's hands for comfort. It could have been a scene straight out of some play I thought, as the whole thing took on a nightmarish quality.

But this was no make-believe, and I was aware now of only one person. Furious, blazing, accusing, Bron's face was a study of incredulity, anger and bitter hurt. 'Oh, Vicky, how could you!' he cried in despair, raising one hand to his forehead and raking fingers through his hair. And at this point I began to think that surely he was over-reacting, for yes, it was a nuisance that the stills were spoiled, but they were only stills and surely he could reproduce another set without too much trouble. Then as my wobbly legs began to work again and I drew closer, my heart sank again.

Beside the ruined photographs were standing several large spools of film, which I knew for certain had not been there when I put my coffee down. Now I could see that — oh no! — the hot liquid had seeped into these as well. Bron had snatched up one of them and was holding it away from him while brown gunk dripped relentlessly all over the floor. How could one mug of coffee make so much mess, I asked myself, as I helplessly reached out an ineffectual hand, which he brushed impatiently away. For there was absolutely nothing I could do.

I glanced towards Rebecca and gave her a stony glare. You bitch, I swore under my breath, using language I would never say aloud. You moved those spools when my back was turned. You set the whole thing up, on purpose to drop me in it. To drive a wedge between me and Bron. Now I could fully understand the meaning of the triumphant smirk she'd given me.

Well, she'd succeeded. Bron was now glaring at me, his jaw set, and beneath the tan his face was white and drawn with fury. 'Do you know what this means?' he flung at me between gritted teeth. 'A whole day's filming — ruined — all through your carelessness.' He looked away and his shoulders slumped. 'Just as I thought we'd finished — had the whole thing in the bag — nicely within schedule and budget.'

'And now,' he waved the reel of film under my nose, 'now I've got to shoot this all over again. More money going out — another whole day's pay for everybody — another whole day wasted.' His voice grew husky and he swallowed hard as he added quietly, 'Just when I so wanted this to be a success.' He banged a clenched fist on the table and hurled the ruined film into a corner. Whirling round to face me again, he finished, 'Because you know any future contracts will hang on the outcome of this first one. And I've blown it.'

'Bron,' I began hesitantly, 'I can't tell you how sorry I am, but . . . ' I bit my lip. No way could I tell him what had really happened. Whatever he might think of me, I was no sneak, and even if I were, he would only think I was trying to blame someone else to exonerate myself.

'Sorry?' he exclaimed, 'Pah! Not half as sorry as I am. I guess you'd better get out of my sight Victoria, before I say something I'll regret.' His eyes bored into mine with the force of a laser beam, and something inside me twisted with pain. 'That was scene two that you've ruined, so I shan't need you for the remake. I suggest you go home,' his lips tightened, 'And you needn't bother coming back.'

Without another word, I went. Out through the crowd, some shuffling their feet in embarrassment and avoiding my eyes. Out to the car and away, through a mist of tears which made driving difficult and almost impossible on the twisting road. Once out of sight of the village, I drew up in a lay-by, laid my head on my arms over the steering wheel, and broke down in a flood of tears.

When I had cried myself out, I mopped up and headed for home. I went in by the shop door which was standing open and was met by a look of surprise by my sister. 'Oh — Vicky — you're soon back.' She must have noticed something about my face, probably there was a lingering redness around my eyes, as she gave me a questioning look and added, 'All right, are you?'

I pasted a smile onto my face and nodded. 'Yes, fine. The filming's finished, that's all.' I skirted the counter, heading for the stairs.

'Oh, I see,' she replied as she busily stuck an adhesive price label onto the top book of a pile in front of her. 'So when will you be seeing Bron again, then?'

I shrugged as nonchalantly as I could

and said casually, 'Oh, we've nothing planned. Was there any post for me?' I changed the subject as quickly as possible and Diane picked up two or three envelopes and handed them to me.

'Here you are,' she said, 'but they all look like junk.'

I glanced through the letters as I climbed the stairs to the flat. Three of them certainly were junk mail, but the fourth was from my agent. Tossing my bag into a corner of the living room, I sat down on the sofa with my feet up and slit it open. Then in spite of my depression, my spirits lifted a little as I scanned it. Apparently the firm who had commissioned the wild-life calendar were now offering me another assignment. They wanted me to do a series of photographs of the old mining remains up around Camborne and Redruth, for a forthcoming article in a local magazine. And the fee they were offering was considerable enough for me to jump at it.

I swung my legs to the floor and reached for the phone. I must make sure I accepted this right away before it was opened to anyone else. It was too good a job to miss and besides, it was just what I needed to take my mind off everything and everyone at Zennor.

Glancing at the clock, I realised that Diane would be shutting up the shop soon, so I wandered into the kitchen and began putting things together for lunch. Over the meal I told her about the commission, and this kept the conversation going without referring to anything more personal. In fact she appeared to be slightly withdrawn herself, but shook her head when I mentioned it. 'No, it's just the thought of stocktaking time coming up,' she replied with a smile, so I shrugged. I knew what an upheaval that was, and that she usually took on temporary help for a few days over the busy period.

In the afternoon I went through the finer details of what was required by the magazine, and then walked into Penzance to get in a stock of batteries for the camera. I certainly didn't want to run out when I was up in the wilds of the mining country.

\*   \*   \*

Next morning I drove up to the grey industrial area that was Camborne and Redruth, a district once teeming with activity until the collapse of tin and copper mining around the eighteen-sixties. Now apparently the last tin mine in Cornwall had just closed, and the magazine was going to run a feature about it. How it would be the end of an era of two thousand years of continuous copper and tin production. And how since then, Cornish hard-rock miners had taken their skills across wider seas and had achieved international fame for their expertise. So they wanted me to come and record the remaining evidence of where it had all started.

Now as I followed a tortuous track

up a slope overhung with gorse and heather, all around me reared the gaunt skeletons of huge buildings. They punctuated the treeless moorland, their ancient chimney-stacks pointing impotently heavenwards.

These were the 'Cornish castles' — the bare bones of former beam-engine houses which had served the once-great mines. Winding engines, pumping engines and the stamps which pulverised the ore with their heavy iron feet.

But a soft drizzle had begun to fall and I looked impatiently skywards. Rain was the last thing I wanted. However, the mist was closing in regardless, and the great houses loomed eerily out of it like stone giants pointing their petrified fingers forever to the sky. It was quiet here, the sounds of civilisation swallowed up in the fog, and without being fanciful, I felt that the hillside suddenly seemed peopled with ghosts. It wasn't difficult to imagine the hundreds of miners whose hob-nailed boots had clumped along this track on the way to work every day. I raised my eyes to the top of a chimney and the cloud cover could have been smoke rising from it.

My imagination had really taken hold now and I stopped where I was for a moment, almost hearing the hiss of steam, the shout of men's voices on the wind, the clang of shovels on metal as the boilers were stoked, and the rhythmic pulse and throb of the engines at work.

Being Cornish-born, I knew something of what their lives had been like, these hardy men who spent their entire working lives in the slimy darkness hundreds of feet below the surface.

Starting underground as young as ten, full of excitement and enthusiasm at being one of the men, those eager boys could look forward to a life shortened by lung disease and appalling accidents. And those who survived, fortified by their 'croust' of pasty and cold tea, had to cope with the chancy 'boom and bust' economy around

107

which mining inevitably involved.

I shook myself back to the present and continued up the hillside. A breeze had sprung up now and thankfully, was beginning to send the mist scudding away eastwards. It had only been low cloud after all, and a strip of lighter sky was becoming visible already. I took out my camera with a sigh of relief, and began doing the job I'd come for.

Now with the wider vista opening up, I could see that some of the formerly crumbling engine houses had been stripped of their layers of ivy and overgrown vegetation and made safe. Not exactly rebuilt, but their decay had been arrested, and information plaques now stated what the purpose of each one had been.

I found myself walking too, on a newly-laid trail of fresh gravel which according to the information boards, linked the mining sites in a comprehensive fashion. Funding from Europe and various other sources has enabled the area to be developed into an attractive venue for visitors without losing its original character, and it had recently been awarded World Heritage status. This then, was what the magazine article was going to be about. Now I understood, and spent the rest of the day taking shot after shot of this atmospheric place.

Then I sat on the summit of a breezy hill and stared out over the mine workings below, towards the sea that was just visible in the distance. I let my thoughts wander, and of course I couldn't get that morning's incident out of my mind. The injustice of it, the sheer nerve of the woman, the malice which drove her, and Bron's agonising rejection of me, all seethed round and round in my head until I thought I would burst with frustration.

But there was nothing I could do to change things. I sighed wearily and reached for my belongings. I'd lost all sense of time and had no idea how long I'd been sitting there, but it was getting chilly and the sun had begun slipping westwards down the sky. I shivered and rubbed at my arms. It was time to go home.

I spent most of the following day viewing my photos, deciding which were the best ones to keep and deleting the others. By the time I'd done that, then put the memory card into my computer and printed them out, I'd had enough of work. I was quite pleased with the way they'd turned out, and hoped the magazine editor would be too.

'How's the stocktaking going, Di?' I asked as I drifted downstairs and into the shop with the vague idea of getting myself something to read for later on.

My sister raised a flushed face from where she was kneeling at the bottom shelf of a tall stack and ran a dusty hand through her hair, 'slowly and painfully,' she replied, half-joking as she straightened up and rubbed her knees. 'I'm on my own — Michael's ill and can't come in.' She shrugged and spread her hands wide. 'But it has to be done. Because now I've started I've got to finish it, else the whole operation is a waste of time.'

What could I say? Of course I would have to help her out. So that's what I did for most of the following day, and together we made such good progress that by mid-afternoon when we made a break for a cup of tea and a rest, Diane gave me a hug and said, 'Oh, Vicky that was fantastic! I can't thank you enough — I am so grateful for your help. I don't know what I'd do, little sister, if you weren't around to prop me up!'

'Oh, that's OK, big sis,' I replied with a smile, 'we've always been there for each other over the years, haven't we?' And again the perpetual problem surfaced — what was I going to do with the rest of my life? More than ever I wanted to move out, get a place of my own, make a fresh start, now that my friendship with Bron was all washed up. In all probability I would never see him again, and my throat tightened. But it might have come to nothing in any case.

Now however, looking intently at my sister without seeming to, I became aware of the tiny worry lines around her eyes and forehead, which surely had not been there before? But how often had I looked at her recently? For weeks I'd been spending the minimum amount of time at home and as much as I could down at Zennor, obsessed with a man who had eventually turned his back on me and left me as high and dry as flotsam from the tides.

That Diane had certain problems, I knew. It was becoming increasingly difficult to run the shop at a profit, particularly in the winter months. Bills for food and services were inexorably rising and I knew that without what I contributed to the housekeeping, she would have even greater difficulty in making ends meet.

With a sigh I sat down and put my feet up on a pile of books, then pasted a smile on my face and raised my mug of tea in a mock salute. 'To us!' I said. And nearly choked as the shop bell tinkled, the street door opened and Bron walked in.

# 6

My hand shook, hot tea splashed my knees, but I hardly noticed as I jumped to my feet in astonishment. My heart was hammering and my legs, I was furious to find, had suddenly turned to jelly.

Diane was the first to speak, greeting Bron perfectly normally, for of course she had no idea of what had happened the other day. While they were exchanging the usual pleasantries about the weather, and Diane was offering tea which Bron declined, I managed to pull myself together, stop shaking and say coolly to him, 'Well, Bron, this is a surprise.'

As I raised my head to meet his eyes he looked swiftly away and I realised that he actually seemed to be embarrassed. I was just taking this in as he carefully wiped his feet on the doormat for the second or third time, cleared his throat and said briefly, 'Vicky, can you spare a few minutes? I need to talk to you.'

Widening my eyes in surprise, I nodded. Then, not wanting to seem too eager, although I was dying to know what all this was about and could hardly believe he was actually there and was not some mirage conjured up by my thoughts, I replied slowly, 'I think a few minutes would be OK. Is that all right with you, Diane?'

'Of course it is,' she said heartily, 'You know we're just about finished here.' Which rather took the edge off my grand gesture.

'I thought — er — perhaps we could go for a walk,' said Bron, his hand already on the door handle.

'Oh, right. Fine,' I replied, brushing dust off my jeans as I crossed the room. 'Where shall we go?' I asked as we turned down the street towards the harbour.

'Oh — I don't mind. Anywhere will

do,' Bron replied, running a hand abstractedly through his already tousled hair. 'Along the prom, then.' He indicated with a hand and we walked on in silence as I wondered what all this could possibly be about. It must be something pretty important to make him leave his film set and drive all the way over here.

'Let's sit down,' Bron said abruptly as we reached an open-fronted shelter where there was, surprisingly considering the crowds thronging around us, an empty seat. We sat facing a sea of sapphire blue over which gulls were dipping and soaring like pieces of torn paper, and where to our left, the Mount sat majestically in all its summer splendour.

Bron was sitting with his head bent, fore-arms resting on his knees and was awkwardly twisting his fingers together as he began to speak. 'I don't quite know how to put this, Vicky,' he said at last, 'but I owe you the most tremendous apology.'

My head jerked round and our eyes met as he looked up at the same time. 'Apology?' My voice came out as a squeak as I struggled to take this in. Whatever I had expected, it was certainly not this. 'What for?'

Bron was looking down at his hands again as he drew in a deep breath and went on. 'About the other morning,' he muttered. 'When I bawled you out. Without letting you say a word in your own defence.'

'Oh,' I said and waited, my gaze fixed on the bent head beside me, and in spite of everything, it was all I could do to restrain my treacherous body from putting out a hand to stroke that unruly mop of hair. Broad shoulders flexed beneath the white polo shirt as he paused for the right words. Then, 'It was unforgivable of me,' Bron said at last, 'and it took a child to put me right.'

'A child?' I echoed again, parrot-fashion, and felt a frown crease my forehead, 'I don't understand.'

Bron heaved a sigh and spread his hands expressively. 'It's a long story, Vicky, but hear me out before you say anything. You see, Isabel and her brother were playing hide and seek, and she came in shortly after you and hid underneath the table where the films were. She had seen you put down your coffee and leave the room. Then she saw Rebecca's feet — she said she recognised her by her shoes — and she heard her moving things around on the table above.'

I was listening in astonishment, my mind in a whirl, but having been told not to interrupt, by a great effort of will I kept my mouth shut and fixed my gaze on the golden arc of sand that was Marazion beach, as Bron went on.

'Then,' he said, 'when Isabel took a cautious peep to see if Sam was anywhere around and likely to find her yet, she saw Rebecca tip your mug over, so Isabel ducked back again quickly. She knew how short-tempered the woman could be and was afraid of what

Rebecca would do to her if she caught her spying.'

This was getting more and more surprising — I had had no idea what was going on that day, literally under my feet. I listened intently, for all that I appeared to be watching the white sails of the yachting club gracefully skimming the water around the Mount.

'So,' Bron was saying, 'when all hell broke loose Isabel was trapped under the table all the time, not daring to show herself in case she got blamed in some way. Poor little kid, she was almost in tears by the time she got through telling me this story.' Bron paused, then his gaze met mine as he added, 'But Vicky, she thinks the world of you, you know. She said she couldn't just keep quiet and let you take the blame for something you didn't do, so she plucked up courage — and it must have taken some courage — to find me later on and tell me the truth.'

I let out all the breath I didn't know I'd been holding, in a long sigh. 'Oh, the dear of her!' I broke in, using the old Cornish vernacular expression. I couldn't help interrupting, but Bron hadn't finished yet.

'Well, as you can imagine, I was pretty well knocked out by all this, and I went storming off to find Becca. Of course she blustered and denied all knowledge, said the kid was lying and how could I possibly take the word of a ten-year-old child against hers. Then she tried the tears and pleading bit, but when I threatened to call the cast together and make a public issue of it, she eventually caved in.'

Bron's face was grim and pale beneath his tan as he turned towards me and straightened up as he finished, 'so I sent her packing and told her not to show her face around here again.' I didn't enjoy doing it, Vicky — I hate bad feeling between people, but she was just impossible — way out of order.'

I felt something inside me lift a little at this news, but my mind was really on my saviour, Isabel, and what a debt I owed her. 'Oh Bron, that dear little girl!' I exclaimed. 'I must go and see her and say thank-you. Do you know where she lives?'

He nodded. 'Yes, up around Alverton way — it's not far. I'll take you if you like. Now, if that's OK.'

'Oh — yes, yes, that would be lovely, thanks. I'd like to get her a little reward of some kind — it's the least I can do after her loyalty to me.'

'Well, there's the arcade,' Bron pointed towards a flight of steps, 'I'm sure you'll be able to find something in there.' As we strolled together towards the shops I almost had to pinch myself to make sure I wasn't dreaming. It felt surreal, after only this morning I'd been thinking I'd never see him again, and here we were together, part of the summer crowd, looking for all the world just like any other young couple on holiday.

Finding something pink and girlie that would appeal to a ten-year-old wasn't very difficult and we left the shop with some assorted jewellery and hair adornments, plus a small toy for Sam so that he wouldn't feel too left out.

We were both a little quiet and subdued as the car drew out of the town and up the hill. Then I said, 'Bron, I've been thinking about Rebecca and wondering what happened in her life to turn her into such an unpleasant character.'

'Mm,' he grunted, negotiating a busy roundabout, 'from what I've gathered, she was the only child of elderly parents who doted on her, pandered to her every whim and succeeded in spoiling her rotten. Then when she became an adult and found that all the world wasn't like that, it soured her and made her like she is now.'

'Sad really,' I pondered. 'Oh, are we there?' as the car began to slow down. Bron nodded. 'Yep, this is it.'

'I hope they're at home after all this,' I remarked as the car drew up outside the house and we stepped out. 'I should think it's highly likely,' Bron replied, consulting his watch, 'school started today, and it's after four, so they've had time to get back.'

'Of course — I'd forgotten we're in September now,' I replied, as I unlatched the gate. At that moment the door opened and there was Isabel running down the path to meet us, dark hair flying out behind her. 'Vicky!' she called, her face wreathed in smiles as I bent down to give her a hug. 'Hello, Bron,' she grinned.

'Hi there, you.' He ruffled her hair affectionately, and said, 'Isabel, listen a minute. I've just been telling Vicky what you told me, about the other day.'

The child's face fell and she bit her lip. 'I was telling tales,' she said, and scuffed a foot in the gravel of the path. 'Mummy says it's not nice to tell on people.'

'Darling,' I broke in, 'this time it was the best thing in the world you could possibly have done and you were absolutely right to do it.'

Isabel brightened. 'I don't like Becca,' she said with a pout. 'She pinched me once when we were acting, because she said I was wriggling. But there was an ant crawling right up my leg, that's why. You'd wriggle if an ant crawled on you, wouldn't you? And I bet she would too.'

As we both burst out laughing, Margaret came out of the house and followed her daughter down the path. 'Hello Bron — Vicky — won't you come in? Isabel, where are your manners? We don't keep visitors talking at the gate.'

'It's all right — we've only just got here,' I replied as we all filed indoors.

'A cup of tea?' Margaret asked. 'Isabel — go and put the kettle on, please.'

'Oh, no, no, thank you,' I said hurriedly, raising an eyebrow at Bron who shook his head and added, 'We only popped in just for a minute to see Isabel.' He looked in my direction.

'Yes,' I said on cue, bending down to

the child and passing her the parcel. 'Because I wanted to thank you so much for speaking up like you did. There's a little present for being such a brave girl. And this is for Sam,' I smiled as the little boy appeared, 'because if he hadn't been playing hide and seek with you it would never have happened — and Bron would still be cross with me!' I smiled up at the tall figure above me and he burst out laughing, but behind his eyes was a lingering expression of — what? It was difficult to be sure, as it passed so quickly, but it had been something deeper than mere passing amusement.

We left the children squealing with delight over their gifts and made our farewells, with polite promises to keep in touch, although I could not see this happening in practice. The only thing that connected us had been the filming, and now that was over. And Bron? I stared at the chiselled profile at my side without seeming to as we drove away, and wondered. Where did that leave him now — or strictly speaking, where did it leave us, I thought wistfully.

'We could have a walk on the beach before we go back, if you like.' Bron broke in on my train of thought as he indicated the long strand of Marazion directly below us as we came down the hill. I felt my face light up as I enthusiastically agreed. For I would have willingly taken a walk anywhere with him — along the railway sidings or the docks even — if it meant prolonging this easy togetherness which felt so comfortable and so perfectly right.

So we spent a casual half-hour fooling about like children — skimming pebbles over the low waves that slapped half-heartedly at the shore, picking up glistening coloured shells and pieces of sea-worn glass and tossing them away again, and climbing up the rocky outcrops to poke about in the deep, clear pools hidden in their folds.

After Bron had picked up a long streamer of dripping seaweed and chased me across the sand until I could run no more, we both collapsed in a heap at the foot of a wall, doubled up with laughter, and lay there gasping for breath like a pair of stranded fish.

Eventually we recovered ourselves, and now too exhausted to move any more, we stretched out in the sunshine, our backs to the wall, and basked for a few minutes in silence. I had my eyes closed against the glare until a sixth sense told me that Bron was looking at me, and I opened them with a start to find him bending over me, his face very close and moving inexorably closer.

Then with a murmur his warm lips came down on mine, and we both slid down onto the golden sand, which was as soft and gentle as this perfect moment I wanted never to end.

'Oh, Vicky,' Bron groaned as we eventually straightened up, 'I've wanted to do that for so long.' Dizzily I clung to him, every nerve-end aflame, breathing in the smell of him, revelling in the feel of him, my arms wrapped around his lean torso, hardly able to believe what had just happened. It was like a miracle and almost too much to take in.

'You do feel the same, don't you? Tell me you do,' Bron pleaded, his eyes locking onto mine, boring deep, deep, into my very soul, until I was speechless with the wonder of it. I could only nod and smile as I closed my eyes and with a sigh of content, laid my head against his warm shoulder.

'Vicky,' he said later, as we still sat with our arms wrapped around each other, loathe to draw apart, although the sun was rapidly going down and the tide had risen, threatening to cut us off if we didn't move, 'Vicky, I have to go away soon — for good. The job I came to Cornwall to do is all finished and wound up. There's really nothing to keep me here any more.'

Like having an icy shower after a warm and cosy bath, I was jerked back to reality. Of course he would have to leave — I'd been burying that fact deep in my subconscious, like an ostrich with its head in the sand, hoping that by some miracle it would never happen.

But this was real life, where miracles did not happen. Some of the desolation I was feeling must have shown on my face, because Bron put a finger under my chin and whispered, 'Vicky, I love you so much. I've never felt for any girl the way I feel about you. Will you . . . would you consider . . . coming away with me? As my dearest love . . . as my partner . . . as anything. And eventually as my . . . my wife if you'll have me. Please?' All Bron's soul was in his eyes and I felt my heart shatter into tiny pieces. For I knew I had to refuse him.

# 7

I swallowed hard and struggled to blink back my tears as I wondered frantically how I was going to say what I had to say. Then I took a deep resolute breath.

'Bron, I love you with all my heart and soul — more than you can know — and far too much to want to hurt you.' I grasped his hand in both of mine and squeezed it hard, willing him to listen, to believe me, to understand. 'It really tears me apart to have to say this,' I gulped, ' — but — but I can't.' I let my head droop as I shook it slowly from side to side. 'Not any of those things. Please believe me — I want to spend the rest of my life with you more than anything in the world, but it's not as simple as that.'

Bron drew back as if he'd been stung and wrenched his hand free. 'What do you mean, you can't?' he said, frowning. 'If you want to and I want to, what is there to stop us?' He quirked an eyebrow as he added bitterly, 'You're trying to tell me there's someone else, aren't you?' He took a step away and stood glowering at me. 'Dammit Vicky, you could have told me before now, or even hinted!' His eyes clouded and deep hurt showed in the tight lines around his mouth, as he added, 'You two-timing little . . . And here was I thinking you really cared!' He turned on his heel, but not fast enough to hide the quiver of his lips, then folded his arms across his chest and stared implacably out to sea.

'Bron — listen to me!' I pleaded, holding out my hands imploringly, 'Of course I did — do — more than I can tell you. I've just said so, haven't I? And yes — there is someone else — but not in the way you mean.'

'What? What do you mean then?' He swivelled round until we were face to face again. 'What other way can there be? Either there is another man or there isn't, period.' He shrugged his shoulders and looked bemused.

I choked back a sob and replied, 'It isn't another man — it's a woman.' Then at his expression of total astonishment, I realised what I'd said and hastily added, 'I mean — it's my sister, Diane.'

'Diane?' he barked, and the frown deepened. 'I just do not understand. What does she have to do with it? You're over twenty-one and a free agent, aren't you?' He spread his hands wide in bewilderment.

'Bron, I've such a lot of explaining to do. We need to sit down somewhere and really talk. Let's go to that café up there,' I pointed a finger, 'and have a cup of tea while I tell you the whole story.' Although tea was the last thing I fancied at that moment, my throat was so constricted I doubted I would ever be able to swallow again.

Bron grunted, 'OK, and this had better be good.' He was already heading with long strides towards the steps up from the beach, leaving me to run behind as I tried to keep up with him.

'We can sit at that table outside,' I said, panting as we reached the café, 'it'll be more private.'

So I told him the whole story of my early life. How Diane had more or less brought me up and had always been there for me over the years, how much I owed to her for her loving care and how I felt that my first loyalty should be to her now that she was having her own problems.

Bron heard me out, his eyes boring into mine as our tea went cold and he hung on my every word. 'And, you see, I've always felt that her marriage might have lasted if . . . if I hadn't always been there in the way,' I faltered, as my voice petered out and a silence fell, broken only by the careless chatter of people in the distance and the wailing of sea-birds above us.

Bron took in a deep breath and stared appraisingly at me for me a few seconds. Then, 'Victoria Williams,' he said formally, 'you are a grown woman and not a child any longer. Hasn't it ever occurred to you to talk to Diane and actually ask her how she feels, instead of jumping to your own conclusions?' He pushed his cup impatiently to one side and leaned his elbows on the table as he continued to lecture me. 'And secondly, don't you think that by living at home all this time since you grew up, you've already repaid all this burden of gratitude that you naturally felt when you were a kid?'

'Bron,' I said, desperately wanting him to understand, 'You don't know Diane like I do. Of course she'll say to me yes, go ahead and live your own life, because she's that sort of person. She's so completely unselfish she would say what she knew I wanted her to say. Oh, it's so complicated.'

'Oh, for goodness sake!' Bron exploded, thumping a fist on the table and making the crockery rattle, 'It's you who's making it complicated. Do you really intend to stay the way you are forever, clamped to your sister's side and denying yourself a life of your own?'

'Just like you did when your father died,' I retorted, pointing an accusing finger at him. 'I should think you'd understand me better through having been through it yourself.'

'That was a totally different matter,' he said, brushing it airily away and continuing as if I hadn't spoken. 'Hasn't it occurred to you that Diane might well mean what she says, that she might want a life of her own as well, and is too kind to say so? That maybe it's you who's interpreting the situation in quite the wrong way? Because you can't see over the top of this great guilt complex you're carrying around — over something that happened through no fault of your own, years ago?'

And as those steely eyes bored into mine and his persuasive voice drummed through my head, my mind opened on to an entirely new perspective. Did he have a point? Could he possibly be

. . . right? Surely not. But could I talk to Diane? It wouldn't be easy. But if I didn't do something . . . Bron was going away soon . . . how could I live any sort of life if . . . if I lost him?

I licked dry lips. 'Bron — when are you actually going? Where are you going? And how much more time do we have?' I whispered, as head bowed, I shredded the paper napkin in my lap.

'Next week,' he replied roughly. 'Next Saturday.'

I gasped. 'So soon?'

He nodded grimly. 'I'm going up to Stromness to see my parents and have a few days holiday, by which time I shall know whether the Board is satisfied with the film and whether they'll agree to renew my contract.' He lowered his voice as he added, 'And if you haven't sorted yourself out by then, Vicky, this will be our last meeting. I have to go, I promised them and they're expecting me, and I want you to come with me — or at least, follow me up there — I do realise it's very short notice.'

'So, it's up to you.'

Bron's face was like granite and his eyes cold and hard. I could see he meant every word he said. Then he rose abruptly and pushed back his chair, leaving me speechless with suppressed emotions — worry over facing Diane, exhilaration that he wanted me long-term, terror that something would go wrong and he would leave without me . . . 'I suggest we make the break now,' Bron snapped, 'and when you've come to a decision, you know where to find me.' Then he flung some coins down on the folded bill between us and walked away.

I sat there frozen into immobility as I watched his broad back retreating further and further into the distance, before I managed to pull myself together and stagger homewards.

★ ★ ★

Diane was not in the shop when I came in, which was odd in itself — she never left it unattended and it was nowhere near closing time. I shrugged, called her name and went through to the stairs that led up to the flat.

It was dark in the passage after the brightness outside and as I paused for a moment to let my eyes adjust, I heard a muffled sound above me.

Then gasped as I saw her figure huddled on the landing between the first and second flights. 'Diane!' I exclaimed, as I took the rest of the steps two at a time, 'whatever's the matter?'

'She felt dizzy and fell partway down the stairs,' came a male voice, 'lucky I called in when I did.'

'Oh — Michael!' I recognised the person who had been coming in to help with the stock-taking but had been taken ill. Then at the sight of Diane's white face and her obvious pain as she tried to move, my stomach started to churn and my mouth dried with shock. 'Oh, my goodness!' I knelt down beside her and took her cold hand in mine. 'Diane, darling, what have you done?

Where does it hurt?' I said urgently.

'She says she had a dizzy spell and tripped on the top step,' said Michael. 'I think . . .'

Then Diane stammered, 'I kind of twisted my ankle and fell with it under me. It took most of my weight and now it's throbbing terribly — oh what a stupid thing to do!'

'Well, let's get you up and make you comfortable somewhere,' said Michael, putting one arm around Diane's shoulders and the other behind her knees, and hoisting her up, 'then we can have a look at the damage.'

'In here, on the sofa,' I told him, 'thank you so much, Michael,' I added as he laid my sister gently down and brought forward a footstool to raise the injured ankle. 'I could never have managed this on my own. You really have been a marvellous help for both of us.' I smiled.

I looked at him appraisingly for a moment. I'd only seen him once or twice before, registering a big, burly figure with a dark beard and curly hair. Diane had mentioned once that he lived down the street in a flat with his partner, Katy, and that he worked in computers. Now as he smiled at me in acknowledgement, and replied, 'As I said, it was just lucky I happened to call in — I came to see how the stock-taking was going,' I saw how good-looking he was, with gentle eyes and long, sensitive fingers. All this flashed through my head in a second as I hurried through to the bedroom for a blanket and some arnica.

Diane flinched and bit her lip as I dabbed the salve on as gently as I could. 'Oh, it's aching terribly,' she whispered, and her eyes were dark with pain. I knew it must be bad for her to admit it, as Diane was usually so stoical.

'I think she ought to go to A and E.' Michael said in an aside to me, 'and perhaps they'll X-ray it. She may have broken a bone.'

I nodded. I was getting really worried

by now. 'Yes, you're right. Look how it's swelling up.'

'I'll take you both in my car — you can't possibly cope on your own, and it'll be quicker than waiting for an ambulance.'

'That's very good of you — ' I began.

'Nonsense,' he said briskly, as he bent to lift Diane again, 'you go on ahead and open the door.'

I tried to keep up a steady stream of inconsequential chat as we drove to the hospital, to distract Diane from her pain and at one point I remarked casually, 'I've never known you to suffer from dizzy fits before, what brought that on?'

Diane managed a weak smile and shrugged a shoulder. 'I don't know, really. I've been feeling a bit tired lately, and not sleeping well, and I have been slightly worried about the shop, to be honest. It's not doing too well, but the dizziness is nothing. I just got up too suddenly, I expect. Then like a fool I went dashing back downstairs too fast.'

We had to wait for an hour before Diane could be seen, but she was given a couple of painkillers and picked up a magazine to glance through while Michael went to fetch us all a cup of coffee. I sat gazing at the people around us and lost myself in my own thoughts.

If Diane was going to be laid up for long — which seemed highly likely — I was going to be desperately needed at home. Obviously she wouldn't be able to stand for long, or climb the stairs, so running the shop would be out. I would have to take that over, as well as nursing her, and coping with all the household tasks as well — cooking meals, washing, cleaning, the list was endless. And it would be for much longer than one week. Oh, Bron! I clenched my fists until the nails drew blood, and stifled the scream that rose to my throat. For how could I run out on my sister now?

At last her name was called and a nurse brought a wheelchair to take her in to the doctor. Then after a thorough examination and a test for blood pressure she was sent for an X-ray as we had expected, so Michael and I returned to our seats in the waiting room. Another boring hour passed, then at last Diane's chair re-appeared, and now her leg was in plaster from knee to ankle and the nurse with her was carrying a pair of crutches in one hand.

'Miss Williams,' she called to me as she put the brake on the chair and left it at Michael's side, 'the doctor would like a word with you. Will you follow me, please.'

He looked up from his notes as I entered, smiled and indicated a chair. I could feel my legs shaking as I waited for the diagnosis. 'Your sister has broken a small bone in her ankle, but is feeling much more comfortable now that it's been immobilised. She'll remain in plaster for about six weeks and will gradually learn to get about on crutches, but she must not put that foot to the ground, you understand?'

I nodded and swallowed on a dry

throat. 'Yes, of course.'

'As to her general health,' he went on, 'we found that her blood pressure is on the low side and that she's slightly anaemic — which would account for the dizzy spell she tells me she had before the fall.'

He must have seen my brows rise in a question for he said in a reassuring manner, 'However, it's nothing that rest and a good diet won't cure. Red meat and plenty of leafy green vegetables — for the iron content, you know?' I nodded again. 'I've also prescribed some tablets for her to take.' He handed me a white box as he went on, 'You and your sister live together, I believe?'

'Yes, that's right.' I cleared my throat.

'Good,' he smiled, rising to his feet, 'I'm sure she'll be well looked after. Don't let her forget to take her tablets, and get her to eat well and not worry about anything. The resting will come as a matter of course — she can hardly do anything else!' His eyes twinkled as he shook my hand and ushered me to the door.

So that was it, I thought bleakly as I walked down the corridor to the waiting room. Diane was obviously going to be an invalid for several months and any decision about my future had been taken out of my hands in the most unforeseen way.

# 8

The days wore on and we embarked on some sort of routine. Fortunately I was between assignments, although I had applied for a few assignments and was waiting to hear results. I needed the money — we needed the money, so when I had a letter in the post to say that my tender for a particular job had been accepted, I was glad in one way, but was left wondering where ever I was going to find the time and opportunity to do it.

However, as it happened, Michael turned up trumps in an unexpected way. He came round one evening to see how Diane was and we were sitting around chatting, when he remarked, 'I've been trying to think of a way of relieving Vicky from looking after the shop, as well as everything else, and it occurred to me that I might be able to help.'

'Oh?' Both Diane and I looked at him with raised eyebrows.

'Yes, tell me what you think of this arrangement.' He leaned forward, elbows on his knees and went on, 'I could come in each morning on the way to work, carry Diane down the stairs and put her in the wheelchair in the shop. Once there, you could manage to serve and do paper-work, answer the phone and so on, even if you didn't do anything else, couldn't you?' he asked her.

Diane's face lit up as she gave him a radiant smile. 'Oh, that would be fantastic,' she said with enthusiasm. 'I've been feeling terribly guilty at having to sit here doing nothing, while Vicky's running about all over the place trying to do two people's work. Thank you so much, Michael, that's an inspired idea.' He was positively glowing at her delight as he added, 'Then I could take you back upstairs on the way home.'

So that's what we did, which took an enormous burden off my shoulders and now that I was free to go out, I could take on the job after all. My brief was to supply illustrations of the wild life at a nature reserve near Hayle, a few miles up the coast, for a country magazine which was doing a feature on it. It was ideal as it meant I could choose my own hours and fit it in with the household tasks. So I breathed a sigh of relief and set off one morning of cloudless sunshine and a warm breeze fanning my cheek through, the open window of the car.

The town of Hayle had originally grown up around the tidal river of the same name that had made it a thriving port in the heyday of the mining industry which was carried on. Similarly, it had gradually declined along with the demise of the mines, becoming a shadow of its former self.

However, the tidal pool was home to a teeming population of bird life, which was why I was here. I began to look for a good vantage point from which to get some shots before the water came in and walked the length of one side of the pool towards the reed bed at the other end.

There was a straight track here that was formerly a railway line transporting ore from the mines to the quay, and taking back coal for fuelling them. Now all traces of its past had been eradicated and it had been transformed with plants and shrubs, making it a pleasant place for recreation.

The place was alive with birds, making the most of pickings in the rich mud before the tide came in. Dainty white egrets paddled in the shallows around the edge, busy dabchicks and ducks bobbed about in the deeper channel where water still flowed, along with two or three stately swans gliding with the current. As the reed bed came into view I could see a couple of curlews poking about with their curved bills and occasionally giving their distinctive, mournful cry. I settled down to my work.

It was an interesting and demanding assignment and served to take my mind off my own problems while I was occupied with it. But in the depths of the night Bron's face would come back to haunt me, I would hear echoes of things we had said to each other, and as I was tortured by memories of the fun times we had shared, I knew I could never, ever forget him.

I kept on seeing men that looked like him. In the street when I went shopping — every so often a glimpse of a man I could swear was Bron. It might be the tilt of the head, the way of walking, the broad shoulders, or the blond hair. I would increase my pace, my heart fluttering with excitement, feeling sure this time I was not mistaken. Then he would turn round and of course it was always a total stranger.

A week passed, and we were into the second one with time ticking relentlessly away, I was tempted sometimes to go and seek him out, to explain about

Diane's accident so that he wouldn't leave Cornwall thinking that I hadn't made the effort to sort things out with her. But, I told myself, the situation hadn't really altered, only the reason behind it. And as Bron's ultimatum had been quite definite — we don't see each other until I was prepared to go away with him — I reluctantly shelved the whole idea.

I had invited Michael several times to join us for the evening meal after he had brought Diane back, and he usually agreed. I remarked casually to him on one of these occasions, 'Doesn't your partner — er — Katy, isn't it? Doesn't she mind you spending so much time with us? You could bring her one round too one night, you know, if she'd like to come, that is.' His reaction struck me as rather odd, as I'd expected him either to agree, or to reply with a spot of lightweight banter.

But he took a breath, almost choked on the sip of wine he'd taken, and looked distinctly uncomfortable as he grunted, 'Oh — um — no, she doesn't. And thank you, but — er — no, she won't come round.' I gave a mental shrug, thought no more about it then, and changed the subject.

Later, after he'd gone, I said to Diane as we sat in the window as darkness fell, watching the twinkling lights come on around the bay, 'What did you say Michael does for his work, Diane? Computers, is it?'

'Yes, he manages a business in Penzance, selling and servicing. He does quite well I think and has several staff under him.'

I nodded. 'Oh, yes. He always looks expensively dressed, and that great car he drives must have cost a small fortune.'

A comfortable silence fell as we watched a couple of tiny boats come chugging round the point, out of Newlyn or Mousehole for the night's fishing. 'You're managing OK in the shop, are you?' I asked Diane, as I collected up the empty coffee cups.

'You don't find it too tiring?'

'No, I find I can do most things now that I've got used to manoeuvring the wheelchair. The leg doesn't hurt at all with the plaster on. Just itches a bit sometimes. I took a big order today actually.' I raised my brows enquiringly. 'A travelling Shakespearean company is doing a tour down here apparently. They're playing at the Hall for Cornwall. Their producer came in this morning and wants twenty-five copies of *A Midsummer Night's Dream*. He couldn't find any in Truro. Good for business, eh?' she said happily.

Diane went rattling on about the rest of her day but I hardly heard her. My mind was back in my own midsummer dream — down at Porthcurno with Bron, beside the whispering sea, my senses lulled by the scents of honeysuckle and thyme as they wafted about us on that lovely day.

★ ★ ★

The week soon slipped away and I realised with a stab of pain that Saturday had crept up on me already. The Saturday when Bron would be leaving, having heard nothing from me and therefore assuming the worst — that I didn't love him enough to make the break with my sister.

I threw myself into my work all that day, forcing myself to concentrate on the job and think of nothing else. But I had to go home sometime, and I had to stop thinking about Bron. He would be well on his way by now and I was going to have to face the rest of my life without him. I climbed the stairs on legs that felt like lead and put a false smile on my face as Diane greeted me.

She was becoming increasingly proficient at getting around on her crutches, and was able to do simple tasks where she could sit down, like washing dishes or peeling vegetables, after Michael had brought her upstairs in the evenings. This was a good help to me when I came in from work and meant that we could eat a deal earlier than if I had to start from scratch.

But when Diane said cheerfully, 'Oh, Vicky, Michael's eating with us tonight,' as I came in and dumped my photography stuff in a corner, my heart sank. The last thing I felt like was company and having to make polite conversation with a visitor. 'That's OK, isn't it?' she added, turning towards me. 'I'm doing some extra vegetables, but I can't remember what you said we were actually having.'

Really irritated now, as I'd only taken two steaks out of the freezer that morning, I sternly reminded myself of all that Michael had done for us. But he'd been joining us more and more often lately — I shouldn't think he had a home of his own to go to.

Muttering under my breath, I grunted a reply that I hoped sounded agreeable. I would just have to de-frost a third steak, wouldn't I? Oh, well, I suppose it wouldn't take long in the microwave. I sighed, I'd been looking forward to a relaxing evening and had been planning to show Diane some of the shots I'd taken, to keep my thoughts from straying elsewhere.

But I made a conscious effort to be sociable and the meal passed pleasantly enough. Until I rose to put the coffee on and Michael said, 'We won't, thanks all the same, Vicky. I'm taking Diane out for a drive — it's such a lovely evening — and we may go for a drink afterwards. I thought it would make a nice change for her.'

I had been staring open-mouthed at them both, wondering why on earth Diane hadn't mentioned it to me before now, when I noticed her heightened colour.

What on earth was going on? If I didn't know he had a partner already I should have said that Michael was smitten, and by Diane's flustered appearance, that it was mutual. But I must be mistaken.

'Oh well — yes — sure. Have a nice evening, both of you,' I managed to stammer, as Michael hoisted her into his arms and headed for the stairs. 'I'll bring the crutches and open the door, shall I?' I added. Diane gave me a grateful smile and said something inconsequential, and soon after that I heard the car draw away.

It was late when they got back — I was in my night clothes reading in my bedroom, not dreaming for a minute that Michael would stay after he brought Diane up. But I heard her calling my name and with a sigh, I put down my book and came through to the lounge.

They were sitting together on the settee. I could sense the air of suppressed excitement about them as soon as I entered the room, and felt my eyes widen.

'Oh, Vicky,' Diane said, holding out her hands to me, 'come and sit down. Michael and I have something to tell you.' I went across to join them on the three-seater, and even then I didn't guess what was coming. 'Prepare yourself for a shock, darling — ' she took a deep breath, and said, 'Michael has asked me to be his wife, and I've consented!'

Shock indeed — that had to be understatement of the year! I was stunned and my head was reeling so much I could only gawp senselessly at her as I felt my jaw drop. Whatever I'd expected it wasn't this. 'Say you're happy for us, Vicky?' Diane pleaded, as she obviously noticed my expression and her face lost its radiance.

'Of course I am!' Pulling myself together I hugged her close, then reached to shake Michael's hand. 'Many, many congratulations, both of you. I'm absolutely thrilled to bits,' I added, stretching the truth. For I hadn't actually taken this in yet, and what it would mean to me personally remained to be seen.

I was struggling to recover my wits, and having regained a little self-control, I asked, 'So, tell me all about it, you dark horses, and why you kept it such a secret that I didn't have the faintest idea what was going on.'

'Ah, well, that was my fault,' Michael replied, crossing one well-creased trouser leg over the other and reaching for Diane's hand. 'As you may or not know, I had a previous partner — Katy — with whom I lived for several years. But about twelve months ago that relationship began to get slightly rocky. I won't bore you with the details,' he waved a dismissive hand, 'but eventually she told me she'd met someone else and wanted to move out.' He shrugged. 'I didn't object as I knew we'd come to the end of the road, so I've been living alone for the last two or three months —'

Now, as this story unfolded, I could see how the liaison with Diane had come about — I knew how Michael loved books and could understand how lonely he must have been after Katy left. He came to help in the shop at weekends, he and Diane got to know each other better

'— until Diane kind of threw herself

into my arms by falling down the stairs,' Michael finished.

'In a funny way,' Diane chipped in, 'it was the best thing that could have happened, as Michael was too shy to say how he felt about me before that!'

Michael rose to his feet and went to open a bottle of wine that he'd brought in with him. 'Champagne!' he announced, handing around the glasses, 'a celebration of this marvellous occasion, which I never dreamed would happen!' As we raised our drinks in a toast and I renewed my congratulations, my mind was working overtime. What of the future? Mine as well as theirs. And why, oh why, I wailed inwardly, could this not have happened last Saturday.

'So, tell me all about your plans,' I said, when we'd calmed down again. 'Where are you going to live?' Ungraciously, my inner self was saying, surely he's not going to move in here, is he? Pleasant though Michael was, I didn't fancy playing the eternal gooseberry again, like I had during her my sister's first marriage.

'Well, Vicky,' Diane began, reaching for my hand and giving it a squeeze, 'there are going to be some big changes. We've decided to sell up the shop and move to somewhere of our own, not far away — we've seen a little terraced house we like. It's really pretty, overlooking the sea in Marazion.'

'I see.' I nodded while trying to take in the implications of this.

'As for you,' she went on, 'this flat could be easily made self-contained by blocking up that doorway to the stairs,' she pointed, 'and you could carry on living here if you wanted to.'

How she — they — had got it all wrapped up! It was all a fait accompli already. Without me having an inkling as to what had been going on right underneath my nose. Resentment flared in me for a moment as I thought how close we had been, Diane and me, and she hadn't said a word about all this. But it sank without trace as I gazed at their rapturous faces.

'Vicky, I know how much you've

wanted a place of your own for a long time, but have been too considerate to mention it, knowing how much I depended on you.'

She had? My jaw dropped again. How?

'And I've always felt slightly guilty over that,' she added, reaching for my hand and giving it a squeeze. So Bron had been right all along! Oh, Bron, I cried inwardly, it's all happening too late!

After Michael had left, we talked and talked into the small hours, and when I did eventually get to bed I couldn't sleep, I was so churned up inside. Oh, it's just not fair! I wept tears of frustration into my sodden pillow. How could fate have been so cruel as to make this happen only such a few hours too late — before Bron had even reached the border!

But nobody said life was ever fair.

# 9

Next day my nerves were in shreds and I couldn't settle to anything, but found myself wandering aimlessly round the flat in a dream, picking things up and putting them down again. I was expecting some remark from Diane, but she was too wrapped up in her own blissful dreams to notice me, thank goodness. It would be too complicated to even attempt to explain what had happened, and I could never bring myself to do such a thing to my sister, let alone spoil her own new-found happiness.

Thankfully, Michael called in the afternoon and they went out for a drive into Marazion to look over the house, leaving me free for the rest of the day. And what should I do with it? I had no idea.

I spent some time leaning on my

elbows and gazing out of the window. It was only October but the sky was overcast. Its blank greyness did nothing to raise my spirits. Neither did the sea, which was the colour of gunmetal, the Mount looming a darker shade above it. The tide was out at its farthest point and small waves were slapping half-heartedly at the shore.

Banks of seaweed had been cast up by the tide and gleamed wetly in the distance, where children were frolicking in and out of the water. A few hardy tourists were walking along the causeway towards the Mount, intent on climbing to the castle at the top. In the tiny harbour below, small boats were rocking gently as they waited to take them back after the tide had risen.

I sighed and turned away. I had work to do on the computer, sorting out my files and weeding out stuff that I'd finished with. It was a boring job that I'd been putting off for ages, but this whole day was boring in general. It seemed an appropriate time to get round to doing it.

After an hour the job was done but by then I'd given myself a headache. I needed fresh air. I knew there was a list of shopping to be done hanging in the kitchen where we always kept a memo pad.

None of it was very urgent but I might as well walk up through the town to clear my head and get the shopping done at the same time.

'I took my time strolling up the steep hill past the statue of Sir Humphrey Davy that dominated the street. He had been responsible for inventing among other things, the miners' safety lamp. As far as Cornwall was concerned this had been far and away his most important innovation. For it had meant an end after hundreds of years to the candle traditionally stuck to their hats with a lump of clay.

I glanced up at the great man and turned for home again, laden with my purchases. I thought I'd been out for ages, but the clock seemed to be standing still and there were still hours of the day to get through yet.

Still too restless to settle, I took the car out and decided to go for a drive. Although my heart wasn't in it, at least it would pass the time. Not knowing where I wanted to go, and not caring much either, I swung left and found myself heading along the coast road. The car seemed to be finding its own way as, sunk deep in my thoughts, I suddenly realised that my subconscious was taking me to the cove of the seals, where Bron and I had first met.

Then it had been high summer, with the wildflowers in full bloom and the apricot scent of gorse wafting on the soft breeze from the sea. Now though, a thin easterly wind was nipping round my ankles, the grass was dry and sere, and the flowers long since over and gone. Today, both sea and sky were a similar pewter grey, with huge purple clouds on the horizon telling of rain on the way.

I shivered and pulled my jacket collar

up over my ears. This had been a bad choice of destination. What had possessed me to come to this exposed spot when I could have stayed warm and cosy indoors at home? Memories of course. Memories that would only torture me, but which I could not resist going over and over, a bit like prodding an aching tooth.

I looked over the edge of the cliff. There were no seals to be seen today. Only surging white water hurling itself against the pitiless granite. The wind was getting stronger, blowing me perilously near the sheer drop. A reef of razor sharp rocks grinned up at me like black rotten teeth. I would climb a bit further down where it was more sheltered.

I took the twisting narrow path down to the ledge where I had had my camera trained on the seals. I smiled to myself even as hot tears welled up and pressed behind my lids, recalling how I had yelled at Bron that day, and how he had turned the tables and made me feel like a complete idiot.

When I noticed that there was someone else already on the ledge, staring out to sea with his back to me, I almost turned tail and retreated. I didn't want to share this precious place with a stranger. But something stopped me and made me take a second look. About the same height, blond hair ruffled by the wind, his stance with hands thrust deep in the pockets of his jeans, reminded me so much of Bron.

But of course it couldn't be — Bron was in Scotland by now. It was only because of my desolation, and the fact that I couldn't get him out of my head, that I was naturally seeing him in a stranger, and hoping against hope, however unlikely it was, plus the fact that he happened to be in this particular spot.

Then the young man moved, and in profile it was quite uncanny how strong the resemblance was. It was in the jaw, the nose, the way he held his head, and now how he hunched his shoulders in

168

just that way Bron had, as he turned to retrace his steps up the path and drew nearer.

Then he raised his head and looked up, straight at me. It was like seeing a ghost. It couldn't be! It was — wasn't it? I shook my head to clear it, the ground swayed, then both hands flew to my face and my legs turned to jelly as I shrieked, 'Bron!' For this was no ghost, but the flesh and blood man I'd thought never to see again.

I skimmed down the rest of the track, slipping and sliding on loose stones, the wind whipping strands of hair into my eyes, heedless of danger, both laughing and crying at once.

'Bron! But how ... why ... I thought you were miles away by now! What are you doing here still?' I cried, feasting my eyes on his beloved face.

The face which had initially lightened as I called his name. Now however, it had closed as swiftly as if a shutter had come down. The eyes meeting mine were cold and blank as pebbles. I faltered and my arms that had been outstretched in delight at seeing him, now fell uselessly to my sides.

'You!' He clamped his mouth into a thin narrow line. 'What happened to last Saturday?' The eyes were animated now but still cold and accusing. 'No, don't tell me.' He held up a hand as I drew in a breath to speak. 'You obviously think more of your sister than you do of me. End of story.'

He hunched a shoulder and turned away to look out to sea again. I swallowed down a lump in my throat that had lodged there at this unjust attack. 'It wasn't like that, Bron,' I said in a level tone.

'No?' he sneered, whirling round and jabbing a finger at me. 'What else could it have been? You knew the arrangement we made.' The anger suddenly left his face as he shook his head in seeming unbelief.

Anger was replaced by an expression of . . . what . . . Hurt? Sadness? Disappointment? Whatever it was it left him looking so vulnerable I longed to hurl myself into his arms and hug it all away.

But I was angry as well. Angry at his too ready assumption of why I hadn't turned up last week. And that he hadn't given me a chance to explain. So I bit my tongue and kept quiet as he ranted on.

'I even put off leaving, in order to give you a little more time. I've been coming here every day for a week.' He spread his hands, palms up and shrugged. 'This was going to be the last time.'

He was looking so bewildered and so upset that I had to relent. All my stern intentions melted away to nothing and dissolved in the wind that was whistling around us.

'Bron, come here, I've a lot to tell you.' I took his reluctant hand and dragged him towards the back of the ledge where a natural cave had been formed by an overhanging slab of rock. We sat beneath it on another flat rock, sheltered from the wind. And there I told him all about Diane's accident, about her and Michael being a couple, and how heartbroken I'd been when I thought it had all come about too late.

And when I'd finished my tale a small silence fell. Then Bron turned towards me and put a gentle finger under my chin, raising my face to his. His mouth came down to mine in a long and lingering kiss.

'Oh, Vicky, my dearest love, I'm so sorry, sorry, sorry! I'm a selfish beast, but it was only because I love you so. I couldn't bear to think we would never be together like this, you see?'

The heaving water pounded against the rocks far below us, blown high into plumes of white spindrift by the strengthening wind. It was exciting, exhilarating, but I hardly noticed. My gaze was riveted on Bron's smiling face and those blue, so blue eyes gazing down at me with love.

'I just couldn't tear myself away without seeing you for one last time! I was hanging on and hanging on trying to pluck up enough courage to come round later and say goodbye. Then tomorrow I really was going back for good.'

'It must have been fate that made me come down here today — I didn't plan to,' I said, as arms around each other's waists, we climbed slowly back to the top. The same fate, I was thinking to myself, that kept me awake all night wailing at the injustice of it! My head was reeling now and I had to pinch myself to make sure I wasn't still dreaming. But the warmth of Bron's body pressed close to mine and those expressive eyes gazing down at me were no dream. He had been given back to me when I had thought all was lost, and my soul was singing for joy.

'Come home with me now,' I said, 'and we can tell them about us. Diane will be so thrilled — I know that deep down she feels she's running out on me.'

Bron nodded as we came to the top

of the cliff, still linked as if we would never let each other go again, and paused to catch our breath.

'But Bron, what about your parents — and the job?' I turned to him in puzzlement. 'I thought you said that they were expecting you.'

'I phoned them and explained I'd been delayed,' he replied. 'As for the job, they were very nice about it and agreed to put our meeting back for a week. I'll break the journey to Orkney at Birmingham and stay a night there. I'll have to make a really early start but it can be done.'

'And when I've packed up the flat and cleared everything here, I'll follow you up and . . . ' I was breathless again after this outburst, but I felt like dancing or skipping, my feet were itching so much to get home and get on with it — to get on with the start of the rest of my life.

I looked up at the tall figure gazing lovingly down at me from those incredibly blue eyes, and tears of happiness misted my own as I thought of all we had been through to bring us to this amazing day, and gave a heartfelt sigh as I whispered, 'Oh Bron, I can hardly believe it — we can be together at last — forever!'

## THE END

We do hope that you have enjoyed reading this large print book.

Did you know that all of our titles are available for purchase?

We publish a wide range of high quality large print books including:
**Romances, Mysteries, Classics**
**General Fiction**
**Non Fiction and Westerns**

Special interest titles available in large print are:
**The Little Oxford Dictionary**
**Music Book, Song Book**
**Hymn Book, Service Book**

Also available from us courtesy of Oxford University Press:
**Young Readers' Dictionary**
**(large print edition)**
**Young Readers' Thesaurus**
**(large print edition)**

For further information or a free brochure, please contact us at:
**Ulverscroft Large Print Books Ltd.,**
**The Green, Bradgate Road, Anstey,**
**Leicester, LE7 7FU, England.**
**Tel:** (00 44) **0116 236 4325**
**Fax:** (00 44) **0116 234 0205**

# VENTURE INTO DESTINY

## Catherine Grant

When Melanie Crighton started her new job as companion to Chloe, Jake Masters' young daughter, it wasn't long before employer and worker became strongly attracted to each other. But this love affair could have no happy ending. Jake's magnetic personality ensured that he had an endless supply of admirers in his life, and Melanie feared that she was to be only one of his many 'affairs'. There was also the problem of his elusive wife Marion to consider . . .

# THE ENDURING FLAME

## Denise Robins

Inside his log cabin, in the Great White Wilderness, young Joanna Grey's father dies, and she's forced to flee from the lecherous Conrad Owen into the icy wilderness. Lost and exhausted, she's found by Richard Strange and they shelter in a cabin where they become trapped by raging snowstorms. And, despite discovering their love for one another, they agree that John should return to his wife. But then, terrifyingly for Joanna alone in the arctic night, Conrad Owen appears . . .